KENT ARTS & LIBRARIES

KT-445-037

REFERENCE COLLECTION ....

005467 6

....

LIBRARY ....

33 Books should be returned or renewed by the last
date stamped above

KCC Supplies Dept.   0 07250 2/70

C 07 0413354

DAYS, WEEKS AND MONTHS

by the same author

HIGHDAYS AND HOLIDAYS
GRAN'S DRAGON
MONDAY MAGIC
TALES FROM ALLOTMENT LANE SCHOOL
HAIRY AND SLUG

DAYS, WEEKS AND MONTHS

MARGARET JOY

Illustrated by Juliet Renny

faber and faber

LONDON·BOSTON

First published in 1984
by Faber and Faber Limited
3 Queen Square London WC1N 3AU
Printed in Great Britain by
Redwood Burn Limited
Trowbridge, Wiltshire
All rights reserved

Text © Margaret Joy, 1984
Illustrations © Faber and Faber Limited, 1984

KENT COUNTY

LIBRARY

394. 2ʊ

CC70413354

British Library Cataloguing in Publication Data
Joy, Margaret
Days, weeks and months.
1. Readers – Days   2. Readers – Months
I. Title
428.6
ISBN 0–571–13171–9

CONTENTS

⸎ ACKNOWLEDGEMENTS ⸎

Verses 16–17 of Psalm 74, quoted on page 11, are taken from the New English Bible, Second Edition © 1970, by permission of Oxford and Cambridge University Presses.

The quotation on page 25 is from *The Wind on the Moon* by Eric Linklater, published by Macmillan Publishers Ltd.

The quotation on page 26 is from "Sam Pig Visits the Moon" in *Sam Pig Goes to Market* by Alison Uttley, reprinted by permission of Faber and Faber Ltd.

The lines on page 36 are taken from "Mothering Sunday" in *The Oxford Book of Carols*, by permission of the Oxford University Press.

The quotations on pages 41 and 42 are from *Kilvert's Diary* edited by William Plomer, published by Jonathan Cape Ltd: reprinted by permission of Mrs Sheila Hooper.

The quotations on pages 44 and 53 are from *Lark Rise to Candleford* by Flora Thompson, reprinted by permission of the Oxford University Press.

The quotation on page 51 is from "Holiday Memory", *Quite Early One Morning* by Dylan Thomas, reprinted by permission of J. M. Dent and Sons Ltd.

The quotations on pages 51 and 55 are from *Cider with Rosie* by Laurie Lee, reprinted by permission of The Hogarth Press.

The lines on page 61 are from "Anthem for St Cecilia's Day"

from *Collected Poems of W. H. Auden*, reprinted by permission of Faber and Faber Ltd.

The quotation on page 79 is from *Unreliable Memoirs* by Clive James, reprinted by permission of A. D. Peters and Co. Ltd.

⸙ THE CALENDAR ⸙

"The day is thine, and the night is thine also,
thou didst ordain the light of moon and sun;
thou hast fixed all the regions of the earth;
summer and winter, thou didst create them both."
Psalm 74, verses 16–17

From the earliest times people have realized the supreme importance of the sun. It gives light and warmth, and makes plants grow, and yet its fierce heat can bring droughts and so cause hunger and death. No wonder that primitive peoples thought of the sun as an all-powerful god.

The moon gave them reassuring light in the dark, and appeared to have some power over the flow of tides. They thought of it too as a god, usually related in some way to the sun. But they realized that the sun and the moon did not just appear at random, but followed regular patterns: cycles. They saw that if they could work out the length of these cycles, they would be able to calculate when the days would be lightest, when they would be coldest, when would be the best time to sow seeds, and so on. They would be able to regulate their farming in the best way.

There were still huge gaps in their knowledge; for instance, it was believed that the sun went round the earth until, in the sixteenth century, the Polish astronomer, Copernicus, published his new theory of the sun being at the centre of the universe. Because of the work of other famous astronomers like Galileo, Isaac Newton and Herschel, we now have a very exact knowledge of the movements of earth, sun and moon.

We know that the **earth** moves in two different ways. Firstly, it turns round on its axis, like a spinning top, once every twenty-four hours. This gives day to each part of the earth in turn, as it moves round into the sunlight, and night, as it turns away from the sun and becomes dark.

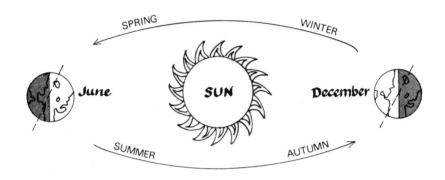

Secondly, the earth travels round the sun in an orbit, taking what we call a year (365¼ days and nights) to go all the way round. Because the earth's axis is slightly tilted, people who live in the northern hemisphere (that part of the earth north of the Equator) have their summer from June to August, when their part of the earth is nearest the sun. The nights are short and the days are long; the longest day is on 21st June. The nearer you live to the North Pole, the longer the summer days, and at the North Pole itself the sun doesn't set at all at Midsummer.

On the other side of the world, in the southern hemisphere (that part of the earth south of the Equator), Australians, for example, have winter in June, when their part of the earth is tilted farthest from the sun. The nearer to the South Pole you live, the longer the night in June. At the South Pole itself, there is no daytime at all at that time of year.

We also know that the moon orbits the earth, taking about 29½ days to complete its journey.

12

The people who lived in **Europe** in the Late Stone Age, about four thousand years ago, knew none of this. They had to try to work it out for themselves. It seems likely that the huge stone monuments in France at Carnac, in England at Stonehenge, and at many other places were built to help them to work out the position of the sun in the sky. These monuments all have a pair of stones which line up with sunrise on the shortest day, 21st December. From this, the Stone Age farmers would have been able to count forward and work out the yearly cycle. So they gradually learnt how to calculate the best time of year to sow seeds, to harvest, etc.

Stonehenge

The **Egyptians** who lived on the banks of the Nile knew only three seasons at first: flood time, seed-sowing time and harvest time. But they realized that they needed to calculate in advance when the Nile was expected to overflow its banks again, so about two thousand five hundred years ago they too began to develop a calendar.

13

They worked out that the earth made an orbit of the sun in about 365 days. They divided their year into twelve months of thirty days, and the rising of the new moon marked the beginning of each month. At the end of each year, five days were left, and these were celebrated as feast days.

In Central America the **Maya** and **Mexicans** also worked out that the earth took about 365 days to complete its orbit of the sun. But they divided this length of time into eighteen months of twenty days each. The "extra" five days were considered unlucky or dangerous, and few people ventured out.

Just over two thousand years ago the **Chinese** were working out their calendar. They too reckoned a year as twelve months of thirty days each. But when the extra groups of five days mounted up to make thirty, they would let an extra thirteenth month into their calendar. (Extra periods of time inserted into the calendar are called "intercalary".)

As well as dividing the year into twelve sections, the Chinese also divided the day into twelve equal periods, and even named the days and the years in groups of twelve. They had names for each of these twelve sections:

tzu (rat), chhou (ox), yin (tiger), mao (hare), chhen (dragon), ssu (snake), wu (horse), wei (sheep), shen (monkey), yu (cock), hsii (dog), hai (pig).

So the Chinese have the hour, the day, the month and the year of the rat, the ox, etc. The year 1984 is the year of tzu, the rat.

The **Romans** followed a calendar which was supposed to have been devised by Romulus, the legendary founder of Rome, about 750 B.C. It was decided that there should be three hundred days in a year, divided into ten months. The first month was called *Martius* (March), after Mars, the god of war, whom the Romans regarded as the father of Romulus. Later, another emperor, Numa, is said to have added two more months and made twelve.

In the first century B.C. the great Julius Caesar, with the help of a Greek astronomer, reformed this calendar, and gave the Romans the so-called **Julian calendar.** This calculated that the earth took $365\frac{1}{4}$ days to orbit the sun, so each year was to have 365 days. Every four years, the four additional quarter days made one whole day, which was added on to February as an "intercalary" day or Leap Day.

Julius Caesar

Gregory XIII

The Julian calendar was used for many centuries, but it finally became clear that it needed reforming. In the year A.D. 1577 two astronomers helped Pope Gregory XIII to correct it. Most European countries, including Scotland, adopted this New Style **Gregorian calendar**; but the English did not accept it until 1751, when it was introduced by an Act of Parliament for "regulating the commencement of the year and for correcting the calendar now in use".

By now Julius Caesar's calculations were eleven days "slow", so eleven days had to be added on to the calendar. It was decided that the day after 2nd September 1752 was to become 14th September. People thought they had been cheated by the authorities, and there were riots, with shouts of: "Give us back our eleven days!"

The same Act decreed that the year was no longer to start on Lady Day, 25th March, the Feast of the Annunciation (when the angel Gabriel appeared to the Virgin Mary and told her that she would become the mother of Jesus). The year was now to start on 1st January. However, the financial year in the United Kingdom still goes by the old practice, so the "tax year" ends at the close of March.

The most recent attempt to change the calendar completely was made by the **First French Republic** in 1793. It was decreed that a new era began with the foundation of the Republic. There were to be twelve months of thirty days each (both days and months being given new names), with five festival days at the end (as in Ancient Egypt). However, this republican calendar was as shortlived as the Republic itself. **Napoleon** made himself emperor and on 1st January 1806 the Gregorian calendar was brought back into use by his command.

In A.D. 1912 the Chinese adopted the Gregorian calendar (although they still give the years the picturesque old names). Until the Russian Revolution, the Russians, Greeks and Turks were still living by the Julian calendar, which was now twelve days "behind" the rest of Europe (so some of the events of the so-called "October Revolution", 1917, took place in the month we call November). Now, however, the Gregorian calendar is accepted and used for international dealings in most countries of the world, though Jews and Muslims still have their own calendars for religious matters, and the forty-five inhabitants of the tiny Shetland island of Foula still celebrate festivals according to the Julian calendar; for instance, they observe New Year's Day on 13th January.

Nevertheless, work to standardize the calendar still goes on. Easter is celebrated on a different Sunday each year. It is always the Sunday following the first full moon after the Spring equinox (20th March). Whitsun also depends on the date of Easter, so it too falls on a different date each year.

16

The Christians of Eastern Europe, who belong to the Greek Orthodox Church, still use the Julian calendar for religious festivals, so their Easter is later than ours. It would be more convenient to celebrate Easter on the same Sunday throughout the world, but so far the World Council of Churches has come to no agreement on this proposed "World Calendar".

A Skipping Rhyme

All in together, girls,
Never mind the weather, girls,
When it is your birthday, please jump IN: January, February,
March . . .

All in together, girls,
Never mind the weather, girls,
When it is your birthday, please jump OUT: January, February,
March, April . . .

The Names of the Months in Different Languages

English	Norwegian	German	Welsh
January	januar	Januar	ionawr
February	februar	Februar	chwefror
March	mars	März	mawrth
April	april	April	ebrill
May	mai	Mai	mai
June	juni	Juni	mehefin
July	juli	Juli	gorffenaf
August	august	August	awst
September	september	September	medi
October	oktober	Oktober	hydref
November	november	November	tachwedd
December	desember	Dezember	rhagfyr

French	Spanish	Italian	Latin
janvier	enero	gennaio	Ianuarius mensis
février	febrero	febbraio	Februarius mensis
mars	marzo	marzo	Martius mensis
avril	abril	aprile	Aprilis mensis
mai	mayo	maggio	Maius mensis
juin	junio	giugno	Iunius mensis
juillet	julio	luglio	Iulius mensis (Quintilis)
août	agosto	agosto	Augustus (Sextilis)
septembre	septiembre	settembre	September
octobre	octubre	ottobre	October
novembre	noviembre	novembre	November
décembre	diciembre	dicembre	December

Esperanto	First French Republic	
Januaro	*Spring:*	germinal (month of germination)
Februaro		floréal (flowers)
Marto		prairial (meadows)
Aprilo	*Summer:*	messidor (harvests)
Majo		thermidor (heat)
Junio		fructidor (fruit)
Julio	*Autumn:*	vendémiaire (wine harvest)
Augusto		brumaire (mists)
Septembro		frimaire (frosts)
Oktobro	*Winter:*	nivôse (snow)
Novembro		pluviôse (rain)
Decembro		ventôse (wind)

The Garden Year

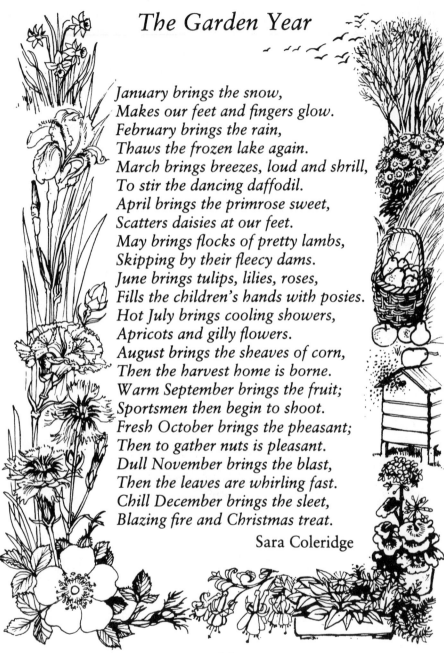

January brings the snow,
Makes our feet and fingers glow.
February brings the rain,
Thaws the frozen lake again.
March brings breezes, loud and shrill,
To stir the dancing daffodil.
April brings the primrose sweet,
Scatters daisies at our feet.
May brings flocks of pretty lambs,
Skipping by their fleecy dams.
June brings tulips, lilies, roses,
Fills the children's hands with posies.
Hot July brings cooling showers,
Apricots and gilly flowers.
August brings the sheaves of corn,
Then the harvest home is borne.
Warm September brings the fruit;
Sportsmen then begin to shoot.
Fresh October brings the pheasant;
Then to gather nuts is pleasant.
Dull November brings the blast,
Then the leaves are whirling fast.
Chill December brings the sleet,
Blazing fire and Christmas treat.

Sara Coleridge

CℐɎ HOW MANY DAYS IN ℭ◯
THE MONTH

English-speaking children work out the number of days in a month by reciting the following rhyme:

> *Thirty days hath September,*
> *April, June and November.*
> *All the rest have thirty-one*
> *Except in February alone,*
> *Which has twenty-eight days clear*
> *And twenty-nine in each Leap Year.*

French, German and Russian children have a different system. They put the backs of their hands side by side and then clench their fists. Months with thirty-one days are those which are counted on the knuckle bones, those months which are counted between the knuckles have thirty days (except for February which has twenty-eight, or twenty-nine in a Leap Year).

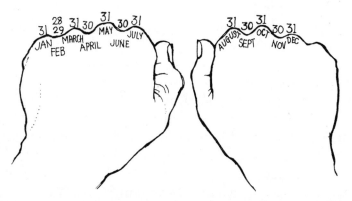

By this system it is easy to see that every alternate month from January–July and from August–December has thirty-one days.

21

❧ THE MONTHS AND ❧ THE MOON

There are two kinds of "moonths" or months, **lunar months** and **calendar months.** "Lunar" comes from the Latin word *luna*, which means "moon".

The moon is comparatively close to us: only about a quarter of a million miles away (very much nearer than the sun, which is ninety-three million miles away). Just as the earth goes round the sun, taking about $365\frac{1}{4}$ days to complete an orbit, so the moon orbits the earth, taking about $29\frac{1}{2}$ days to go completely round; this is a **lunar month.**

There is no such thing as "moon light", because the moon has no light of its own. It shines only by reflecting sunlight. At different times of the month, the moon seems to change shape. These changes are called the moon's "phases". When the moon is in the same part of the sky as the sun, between us and the sun, then its dark side faces us and we cannot see it. When it has moved on a little it reflects a sliver of light; this is the New Moon. By the next night, we can see a slightly wider crescent, and so the moon "waxes" or grows, until half of it can be seen. This half moon is called the first Quarter, because the moon is a quarter of the way along its orbit.

The moon continues to wax until it is on the opposite side of the earth to the sun. Now the whole moon reflects the sun's light, and we call this the Full Moon. Then we say the moon gradually "wanes" or becomes smaller until it reaches its Last Quarter, when we see a half moon again. It goes on waning until it is only a thin crescent, disappears – then we welcome a New Moon back again.

22

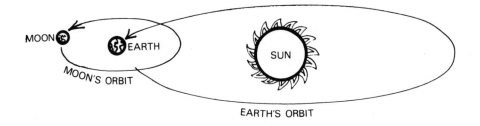

MOON

EARTH

MOON'S ORBIT

SUN

EARTH'S ORBIT

The word "moon" perhaps comes from a very ancient word "mē", meaning "to measure" (like the phrase "to mete out"). People have always used the moon's phases to measure time by. The Egyptians thought the moon was the god Thoth. The Incas said she was Mama Quilla, sister and wife of the sun god. The Greeks too thought she was a goddess: Phoebe, or Cynthia. Norsemen believed that the silver chariot of the night was driven by a youth called Mani. His sister, Sol, drove the golden chariot of the day, and both had to gallop on for ever, since a fierce wolf was pursuing them. The Romans said the moon was the goddess Diana, sister of Apollo, the sun god. It was considered to be of great importance and was mentioned frequently in old rhymes.

Hey diddle diddle, the cat and the fiddle,
The cow jumped over the moon;
The little dog laughed to see such fun,
And the dish ran away with the spoon.

23

There are many beliefs attached to the moon and moonlight. It was considered dangerous to sleep in the open beneath the full moon. A "lunatic" was so called because he was thought to be affected by the phases of the moon. An old proverb runs, "When the moon's in the full, then the wit's in the wane" and the inmates of seventeenth century "Bedlams" (the name given to hospitals for the mentally disturbed) were frequently tied up at the time of a full moon, for fear of its effect. In 1635 someone wrote:

"This disease of lunacie, is a disease whose distemper followeth the course of the moon."

There are many stories of witches, were-wolves and other uncanny beings appearing at the full moon; but there are just as many tales of robbers, smugglers and poachers taking advantage of the moonlight. The famous Lincolnshire poacher sings about poaching:

"...'tis my delight on a shiny night in the season of the year."

Old grandfather clocks were often designed to show the phases of the moon as well as the time of day, as this information was important before the days of artificial light. A full moon could be essential when undertaking a journey by night, a "harvest moon" was of great help to a farmer getting in the last of his crops.

24

The appearance of the moon could be important. A proverb of 1678 advised:

> *"If the moon shows a silver shield,*
> *Be not afraid to reap your field;*
> *But if she rises haloed round,*
> *Soon we'll tread on deluged ground."*

At the beginning of Eric Linklater's story for children called *The Wind on the Moon*, he describes the moon: "...pale and wild, and round it clung a white collar of shining mist." The father of Dinah and Dorinda was worried: "'When there is wind on the moon, you must be very careful how you behave...'" If you read the story you will find out how the wind on the moon affected the two girls.

A new moon was usually considered a lucky sign. The money in your pocket would soon be doubled if it were turned over at the first sight of the new moon. In Somerset you were supposed to say:

> *"New moon, new moon, first time I've seed 'ee,*
> *Hope before the week's out, I'll ha' summat gived me."*

I see the moon,
And the moon sees me;
God bless the moon,
And God bless me.

I see the moon,
And the moon sees me;
God bless the sailors
On the sea.

In one of Alison Uttley's stories about Sam Pig, Sam, like thousands of other countryfolk, bowed three times to the new moon and made a wish – to visit the Man in the Moon. His wish came true, and he found the Man picking up sticks, accompanied by his dog.

"'I like a good fire,' said the Man, rubbing his cold hands before the blaze. 'We only get reflected sunshine up here, so it's mighty cold.'"

He must have been very surprised to see the first Russian *lunik* orbiting the moon in 1959, and even more amazed in 1969 when the first man from earth stepped on to the moon's surface.

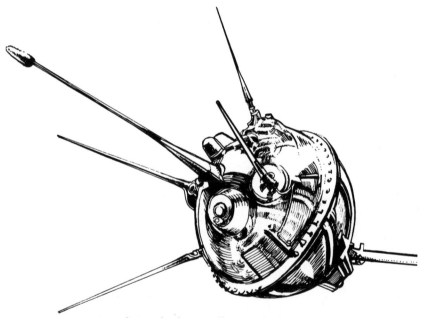

Lunik 2, which actually struck the moon

The second kind of month, the **calendar month,** is an artificial grouping of days. We saw in the section on the Calendar how the Gregorian Calendar, which is now used almost everywhere, was arrived at.

26

ⳇ THE MONTHS ⳝ

January: 31 days

January was named by the Romans after their two-faced god, **Janus**. He was the guardian of doors, entrances and beginnings. Perhaps your school has a "janitor" who looks after the keys of the building and opens the gates; his title also comes from the god Janus.

In the Forum in Rome there was a temple dedicated to Janus. In times of peace the doors were kept shut, but more frequently the Romans were at war somewhere and the doors remained open, ready to receive the victorious army. Janus had a son, Tiberinus, who gave his name to the river Tiber which flows through Rome.

Because Janus had two faces, he could look backwards to the past and forwards to the future, so he was the ideal god to preside over the New Year.

As the first day of a New Year is considered special in every country, people usually celebrate with some sort of party or merrymaking in the hours leading up to midnight. Then the door is opened to let out the Old Year and let in the New, church bells are rung, greetings and good wishes are exchanged, toasts to the New Year are drunk, and in English-speaking countries "Auld Lang Syne" is often sung.

The first day of the New Year is the occasion for making good resolutions for the months ahead. In the eighteenth century an American writer, Benjamin Franklin, advised:

"With the old almanack and the old year,
Leave thy old vices, tho' ever so dear."

The feast of the **Epiphany**, which means "showing forth", is celebrated on 6th January. This reminds us of Jesus being shown forth to the Three Wise Men. In Italy children receive presents on this day. They are said to be brought by an old woman named Befana (a shortened version of the name of the feast, Epiphania). She was said to have started out a day late to look for the Baby Jesus, after the Wise Men passed her door, and she has been searching for him ever since.

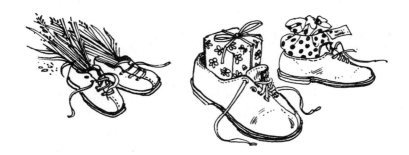

Spanish children leave their shoes on the window-sill with straw inside for the Wise Men's camels; when the children look for their shoes on the morning of Epiphany, the straw is gone, replaced by little gifts — from the Wise Men.

For most of us the sixth day of January means **Twelfth Night**, when Christmas festivities are traditionally at an end and decorations are taken down. However, there is a belief that if you have eaten a mince pie on each of the twelve days following Christmas, the next twelve months should be happy ones.

The day on which work started again after Twelfth Night was known to countryfolk as **Plough Monday**: the day on which labourers had to return to the fields. The day was also nicknamed **St Distaff's Day**: the day on which women had to return to work with the distaff (another word for a spindle) after the Christmas holiday.

The pattern is still being repeated in schools today, as children return to work at the beginning of the new term in the first week of January.

The man in the moon came tumbling down
And asked the way to Norwich.
He went by the South
And burnt his mouth
Eating cold pease porridge.

February: 28 days (29 in a Leap Year)

The name February comes from *Februa*, a feast celebrated by the Romans on the fifteenth of this month. It was a festival of cleansing and purification, and the name for it comes from *februare*, which means "to purify".

In later times the Christian feast of the **Purification** was also celebrated in this month. Held on 2nd February, this feast is now known as the Presentation, since it reminds us of the day on which Mary presented the baby Jesus to be blessed in the Temple soon after his birth. Mary herself was thought to be "purified" by this visit to the Temple after the birth of her first-born. You can read about this in the second chapter of St. Luke's Gospel.

Until recently women still went to be "churched" after the birth of a baby. They lit a candle and gave thanks for the safe delivery of their child. The feast of the Presentation is also known as **Candlemas**, the "Mass of candles", and candles are still lit during services on this day, reminding us that Simeon, the old man in the Temple, told Mary that Jesus was to be "a light to the Gentiles" (non-Jews).

14th February is **St. Valentine's Day**, when it is the custom to send valentine cards, often unsigned, to the person of one's choice. It is a custom which goes far back to Roman times, when young men and girls danced and made merry at the spring festival of Lupercalia, sometimes drawing lots to find a partner.

22nd February is **Thinking Day**, when members of the Scout and Guide movements remember their founders Lord and Lady Robert Baden-Powell.

Shrovetide usually falls in February (though it may come at the beginning of March) and ends on **Shrove Tuesday**, or Pancake Day, the day before Lent begins. During the four days of Shrovetide people used to enjoy energetic and noisy activities, like playing football, skipping, playing battledore and shuttlecock, and smashing old crockery. These wild games seemed to be a way of working the energy out of the system before quietening down for the penances of Lent. Some of these old customs still take place, like the traditional pancake race at Olney in Buckinghamshire; and most people feel it is right to eat pancakes on Shrove Tuesday, although they don't realize that the pancakes were made on this day to use up the rich fat and eggs in the house before the fasting of Lent began.

In some parts of the world, in the Caribbean, the South of France and the Rhineland, for instance, Shrovetide is still a time of colour and carnival, when people "let themselves go".

Lent begins on **Ash Wednesday**. This six-week period is one of preparation for Easter. Its name comes from the Anglo-Saxon word *lencten*, "to lengthen", referring to the days that are now beginning to grow longer. Nevertheless, the weather is often still wintry; perhaps it is a blessing that February is the shortest month. An old saying runs, "February fill dyke, either with black or white" (rain or snow). The Welsh say: *Byr yw chwefror, ond hir ei anghysuron* (February is short, but its discomforts are long). A proverb of 1576 goes: "A faire Candlemas, a fowle Lent." However, there are hopeful signs of spring: crocus buds pushing up and clusters of snowdrops, which have been given various pleasant names, such as "February fair maids", "Candlemas bells" and "Mary's tapers".

31

February normally has twenty-eight days, but every four years we have a **Leap Year** when an extra or "intercalary" day is put into the calendar at the end of February. Every fourth year whose number can be divided by four is a Leap Year (e.g. 1952, 1984, 1992), except century years, which can be Leap Years *only* when divisible by 400. So the year A.D. 1900 was not a Leap Year, but the year A.D. 2000 will be.

It is a long-held tradition that girls may quite properly propose marriage to men in Leap Year, and if the offer is rejected, the girl may claim a silken gown as compensation. In 1288 the Scottish Parliament stated that in a "lepe yeare" any "maden ladye of both highe and lowe estait shall hae liberte to bespeke ye man she like..."

If you have a birthday on 29th February, you share it with a very small percentage of the population. Unfortunately you can celebrate only once every four years!

Sally go round the sun, Sally go round the moon,
Sally go round the chimney pots on a Sunday afternoon.

32

Girls and boys, come out to play,
The moon doth shine as bright as day;
Leave your supper and leave your sleep,
And join your playfellows in the street.
Come with a whoop, come with a call,
Come with a good will or not at all,
Up the ladder and down the wall,
A halfpenny roll will serve us all.

March: 31 Days

In ancient times the year was always reckoned to begin when the new crops started to appear, in what we call springtime. The Romans too began their year in March, so September was their seventh month, October their eighth, and so on.

Until the eighteenth century we also kept this "Old Style" calendar in Britain and North America; then we accepted the "New Style" or "Gregorian" calendar (see page 15) and began the year on 1st January.

The Romans named this month after **Mars**, their god of war. (The Welsh name for this god — **Mawrth** — is still used as the name for both Tuesday and March.) Throughout the bad weather of winter, campaigns had to break off, but in spring fighting could begin again, and so the blessing of Mars was needed.

The Campus Martius was a plain outside the city of Rome. It was a place where the army used to train and took its name from the altar of Mars which stood there.

Paris too has its *Champs de Mars* or "field of Mars". This once-marshy ground near the River Seine was made into a parade ground for the Military Academy in the eighteenth century and named after the pagan god of war. Today you can enjoy taking a walk through the Champs de Mars, as it has been made into a large public garden leading to the Eiffel Tower.

In Shakespeare's day the "martial arts" were still considered praiseworthy. In his play *Richard II* he must have echoed the thoughts of many an Englishman when he described England as:

"This royal throne of kings, this sceptered isle,
This earth of majesty, this seat of Mars..."

An ancient Hindu festival which falls at this time of year is **Huli,** a fire festival which celebrates the new growth of spring. People light their household fires, and then a community fire is kindled by a Brahmin (priest). A figure of Hulika, a legendary character, is placed on the fire to be burnt. Some of the ripe barley crop is offered to the fire, and roasted barley is eaten. Later, a great deal of coloured dust, coloured water and coloured balloons are thrown about, but no one minds if their clothes get wet or stained, as it means good fortune to be sprinkled in this way, and adds to the fun of the occasion.

The Welsh celebrate **St David's Day**, or "Leek Day", as the Reverend Francis Kilvert called it in 1870, on 1st March. The leek is the original emblem of Wales. In Shakespeare's play *Henry V*, a Welsh soldier, Fluellen, says: "I do believe, your majesty takes no scorn to wear the leek upon St Davy's day", to which the king replies: "I wear it for a memorable honour: for I am Welsh, you know, good countryman." (Henry V was born at Monmouth and so could regard himself as Welsh.) However, nowadays a Welshman would probably wear a daffodil or *cenhinen fawrth* (March leek, as it has been nicknamed) in his button-hole on 1st March.

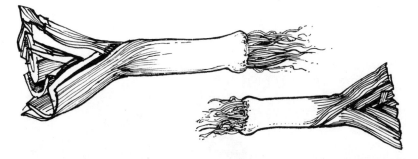

On 17th March many Irishmen wear a bunch of shamrock in their button-holes in honour of their patron saint, **Patrick.**

The **Ides of March** was the name given by the Romans to the fifteenth of March. A fortune-teller warned Julius Caesar: "Beware the Ides of March", but he took no notice and was stabbed to death on the steps of the Capitol on that very day.

25th March is **Lady Day**, one of the year's four traditional quarter-days on which labourers could be hired and rents had to be paid.

The fourth Sunday in Lent, mid-Lent Sunday, usually falls in March. This is traditionally **"Refreshment Sunday"** or "**Mothering Sunday**", when young people who worked as servants were given a day's holiday to visit their families. They often took a bunch of flowers or a cake as a gift for their mothers. In the *Oxford Book of Carols* you can find carols for Mothering Sunday; here are two typical verses:

"It is the day of all the year,
Of all the year the one day,
When I shall see my mother dear
And bring her cheer,
A-mothering on Sunday.

And now to fetch my wheaten cake
To fetch it from the baker,
He promised me, for mother's sake,
The best he'd bake
For me to fetch and take her."

The month of March has a reputation for wildness. John Masefield wrote of "mad March days" at sea. The weather is often squally and windy at this time of year, interspersed with bursts of bright sunshine, so the month is called "March many weathers".

Cattle in the fields are often more skittish and lively in windy weather, and it affects young children's behaviour too. Even hares are said to be "mad" in March (like the "mad March hare" whom Alice met in Wonderland), because they are often seen racing round the fields. It is true that they behave more wildly during their breeding season, which is in the early spring.

If the weather is particularly squally, people say encouragingly, "March comes in like a lion and goes out like a lamb", but they are frequently proved wrong.

The weather doesn't seem to bother sportsmen, particularly those who are spectators — in front of the television set. In March they can watch the Football League Cup Final at Wembley. Later in the month the historic "Grand National" is held at Aintree Race Course near Liverpool.

April: 30 days

The name of this month comes from the Latin word *aperire*, to open. The Romans dedicated April to **Venus**, the goddess of love, fertility and new growth. It is now that buds begin to open. The Greeks and Romans also connected this time of year with the goddess Persephone or Proserpina, who was thought to be released from the underworld each spring, bringing new growth and happiness with her.

The coming of spring is always a joyful time. In the Song of Solomon in the Bible we can read: "For lo, the winter is past, the rain is over and gone; the flowers appear on the earth, the time of the singing of birds is come."

In Northern Europe we cannot always be so sure that "the rain is over and gone". An old saying runs: "April weather, rain and sunshine together." Shakespeare talks of the "uncertain glory of an April day". April showers are proverbial; there is even an old song with that title.

The Spanish say: *En abril, aguas mil* — in April much rain (literally: in April, a thousand waters).

In the fourteenth century Chaucer described a group of pilgrims setting off for the tomb of Thomas à Becket at Canterbury in Kent. He pointed out that the most popular time of year for such undertakings was...

> *"When that Aprille with his shoures sote*
> *The droghte of Marche hath perced to the rote...*

(When in April the sweet showers fall and pierce the drought of March to the root).

Chaucer   The Wife of Bath   The Miller

These "sweet showers" make April an especially fresh and green time of year in this country, particularly as the fruit trees begin to blossom. Robert Browning wrote in "Home Thoughts from Abroad":

> *"O to be in England*
> *Now that April's there,*
> *and whoever wakes in England*
> *Sees, some morning, unaware,*
> *That the lowest boughs and the brushwood sheaf*
> *Round the elm-tree bole are in tiny leaf,*
> *While the chaffinch sings on the orchard bough*
> *In England — now!"*

Some people look forward to a different English happening: the Boat Race between Oxford and Cambridge Universities which takes place on the Thames at the beginning of April.

1st April is **April Fool's Day** in much of Europe. In Scotland an April fool is an April "gowk" or cuckoo. In France children try to fasten a paper fish on a friend's back, unseen, and the victim is then a *poisson d'avril* or April fish, just as in Italy an April fool is a *pesce d'aprile* (April fish).

Numerous reasons have been suggested to account for the custom of playing tricks or sending people on pointless errands on this day. Some say that it is based on the story of Jesus's arrest: he was sent from Annas to Caiaphas to Pilate to Herod. Plays on such religious themes were often performed in market places or on village greens in the Middle Ages, and these incidents in Jesus's last days were the subject of some of the "miracle" or "mystery" plays performed before Easter, near to April Fool's Day.

The six weeks of preparation for Easter are called Lent, and the last week is called **Holy Week**. The Greeks call it *Megali Ebdomada* (Great Week), as the days lead up to the great feast of Easter.

Thursday of Holy Week is called **Maundy Thursday,** when Christians remember the Last Supper. This was the last meal Jesus was to share with his friends before he was arrested. Before the meal he washed their feet, and this symbol of humility and kindness is still imitated today by priests, bishops and even the Pope, when they wash the feet of twelve people in church services on Maundy Thursday.

For many centuries the ceremony was also performed by monarchs, who, after washing the feet of a number of poor people, would then distribute clothing, food and money among them. An account of the ceremony in 1685 reads:

> "On Maunday Thursday, April 16th, 1685, our gracious King James ye 2nd wash'd, wip'd, and kiss'd the feet of 52 poor men with wonderful humility."

Today the reigning monarch attends a Maundy service in one of our cathedrals and then presents the "Royal Maundy" money in purses to as many people as the monarch has years. So, for instance, in 1982 the Queen gave out purses of Maundy money to fifty-six elderly men and fifty-six elderly women.

The next day is **Good Friday**, God's Friday, and recalls the day on which Jesus was crucified. Christian services are held throughout the world on this day; many thousands of pilgrims gather in Jerusalem to worship in the places connected with Jesus's death.

Easter Sunday is a day on which all Christians rejoice in Christ's resurrection from the dead. It is the greatest day in the Church's year. At midnight services the new light of the "Paschal" candle is lit, symbolizing the new life of the risen Christ. From it are lit all the candles of the congregation.

Everyone, Christian or not, feels that there is something

special about Easter. There is even an old belief that the sun dances for joy in the sky as it rises on Easter Day. At Easter it seems that spring has arrived at last, the weather is getting warmer, the days longer. Easter presents, particularly chocolate eggs, are exchanged, and there are two weeks' holiday from school. The milder weather is a good reason for wearing a new "Easter bonnet" or a new outfit. Francis Kilvert noted in his diary on Easter Day in 1870:

> "On Easter Day all the young people come out in something new and bright like butterflies. It is almost part of their religion to wear something new on this day."

Easter Monday has for centuries been a day of fairs or outings, as it is the first official holiday of spring. Nowadays many sporting fixtures take place on this day, and the Easter Parade in Battersea Park, London, attracts hundreds of sightseers.

This time of year is equally important for Jews. They celebrate **Pesach**, the spring festival which commemorates the deliverance of their ancestors from Egypt. This feast is also known as the **"Passover"** which Jesus, as a Jew, was celebrating shortly before his death. Pesach lasts for a week. It begins with the **Seder**, a family meal at which important events in Jewish history are recalled in a traditional question-and-answer ritual, and special foods are eaten.

14th April is called **Cuckoo Day** by countryfolk. It is always rather special to hear "the first cuckoo" of spring.

A baby cuckoo waiting to be fed

41

On 23rd April you may see people wearing a red rose in their button-holes, as the emblem of England, and see the flag of **St George** — a red cross on a white ground — flying above many parish churches and public buildings. It is the feast of St George, patron saint of England. His day was declared a public holiday in 1222, but is unfortunately no longer so. This day is also William Shakespeare's birthday, and the occasion is always remembered in his home town of Stratford-on-Avon in Warwickshire.

The last day of April seems to have been more important in the past than it is today. The clergyman Francis Kilvert, who worked in a parish in the Welsh Border country, wrote in his diary in 1870: "This evening being May Eve I ought to have put some birch and mountain ash over the door to keep out the 'old witch'. But I was too lazy to go out and get it."

In Germany the night between 30th April and 1st May is known as *Walpurgisnacht*, originally named after St Walburga.

This is the night when witches were supposed to ride to the Brocken, the highest peak of the Harz mountains in North Germany. After flying wildly across the skies on broomsticks, tree-trunks, cats' tails and butter-churns, the witches gathered on the Brocken to feast with the devil. Meanwhile the terrified countryfolk protected themselves and their livestock with numerous crosses or branches of birch, and by making as many frightening noises as they could: cracking whips, ringing bells, and so on. With the first cock-crow down in the valley, all spirits and witches and the devil disappeared. Today the Brocken mountain lies inside East Germany, so it is no longer so easily accessible to travellers from western Europe — except to those who can fly there...

May: 31 days

This is the fifth month. It is probably called after the Roman goddess **Maia,** who was thought to encourage growth and increase. In her honour sacrifices were made on the *Kalendae Maiae,* the first day of May, accompanied by considerable merrymaking. At this time of year there has always been rejoicing as summer approaches and crops and livestock flourish. The Anglo-Saxons called this month *thri-milci,* because the grass became more plentiful, and so cows were able to give milk three times a day.

The Celts worshipped the sun. They believed they could encourage his warmth by lighting bonfires at this time of year when they held their feast of Beltane. A tree was often chosen as a symbol of growth and the Beltane festivities took place round it.

At the beginning of May the Romans honoured Flora, their goddess of vegetation and flowers, by decorating a tree or "May pole" and dancing and feasting round it. They brought these customs to Britain, and the maypole became an essential part of the springtime activities.

Preparations for **May Day** on 1st May were made throughout the previous night, when young people would go out into the countryside and return with armfuls of flowers and greenery with which to decorate the maypole and the cottages in the village.

A May Queen and attendants were often chosen to reign over the day's merrymaking, originally representing Flora and her nymphs. In later centuries the Christian Church made links between May and Mary, and then celebrations became religious in tone. Roman Catholics still honour Mary with the title "Queen of the May", and have dedicated the month to her.

In her book *Lark Rise to Candleford*, Flora Thompson describes how children in her village in the 1880s prepared to set out on their May procession, carrying a doll, which they called "the lady", garlanded with flowers. They visited all the large houses in the district; their finery was admired and they were given donations of money. Flora Thompson asks: "Is it possible that the lady was once 'Our Lady', she having in her turn, perhaps, replaced an earlier effigy of some pagan spirit of the newly decked earth?"

1st May is known in Europe as **Labour Day**, a sort of "festival of work". It is a public holiday in some countries, and processions of workers parade through the streets. It has unfortunately become an opportunity for some governments to parade their weapons, as in the May Day Processions in Moscow or Leningrad, often shown on television.

In the United Kingdom the first Monday in May is now a public holiday, called May Day. Around this time football fans await with keen anticipation the F.A. Cup Final which takes place on a Saturday afternoon at a packed Wembley Stadium.

The F.A. Cup

Wesak, the birthday of the **Buddha,** "the enlightened one", is celebrated by his followers at the time of the full moon, at that time of their year which corresponds with our month of May. The Buddha was born a prince, but later he became "enlightened" and renounced his worldly title and possessions. At Wesak his followers remember not only the day of his birth but also his enlightenment and his death.

Ascension Thursday often falls at the end of May. Christians believe that this is the day on which Jesus ascended or went up into Heaven, forty days after Easter. It used to be an important public holiday.

The three days before **Ascension Thursday** are called **Rogation Days,** from the Latin word *rogare* to ask or beseech. Originally these Rogation Days were spent in prayer and fasting in preparation for Ascension Day. At some time during these three days of **Ascensiontide,** processions of parishioners, led by the minister, used to go round the church and the boundary of the whole parish, asking for blessings on the growing harvest. As the processions walked round the parish boundaries, they would recite prayers and often stop at a particular landmark; there are several places in the country still bearing the name "Gospel Oak" for instance. This ceremony became known as "beating the bounds", and was a practical way of making sure each parishioner knew where the parish boundary lay.

45

Feelings are divided about the climate in May. The French have a proverb which suggests that they expect good weather: *"En avril, ne te découvre pas d'un fil; en mai, fais ce qu'il te plait."* (In April, don't remove a stitch; in May do what you like.)

The Spanish, however, are more pessimistic. *"Hasta el 40 de mayo no te quites el sayo."* (Until the 40th May, don't take off your coat: in other words, stay covered up until well into June!) This is rather similar to "Cast ne'er a clout, till May be out (over)". Shakespeare, too, warns that "rough winds do shake the darling buds of May".

Generally, however, people seem to regard this month as "the merry month of May", meaning that it is pleasing or delightful. Thomas Hardy thought so. In his poem "Afterwards" he wrote:

"... the May month flaps its glad green leaves like wings
Delicate-filmed as new-spun silk..."

June: 30 days

This is the sixth month, called after the goddess **Juno**.

Juno was the stately and beautiful goddess of marriage and childbearing, and the patroness of married women. June is still a favourite month for weddings and people speak approvingly of "a June bride", but this may be because of the fine weather we usually hope for in "flaming June".

Whit Sunday usually falls in June. It corresponds with the Jewish feast of Pentecost, which is celebrated fifty days after the Passover, just as **Whitsun** is fifty days after Easter. Pentecost means "fiftieth". It is the day on which the Holy Spirit came down on Jesus's disciples and gave them strength to go out and preach all over the world, and for this reason this day is sometimes known as the "birthday of the Church". Whitsun or

"White Sunday" gets its name from the white garments worn by adults who were often baptised on this day.

The likelihood of good weather is one of the reasons for celebrating the Queen's "official" birthday on the second Saturday in June, even though she was born on 21st April 1926. On her official birthday a Royal Salute of forty-one rounds is fired at 11 a.m. in Hyde Park. Later that day the traditional "Trooping the Colour" ceremony also takes place at Whitehall in London. Riding side-saddle and wearing the uniform of colonel-in-chief of the particular regiment whose colours (or regimental flag) is being trooped, or displayed, the Queen inspects the troops and receives a loyal salute from them.

Racegoers at Ascot

The Queen and other members of the royal family usually attend the races at "Royal Ascot" in Berkshire in mid-June; keen racegoers can also enjoy watching the Derby at Epsom in Surrey — or at home on television. The Lawn Tennis Championships begin at Wimbledon in late June, and all gourmets and gardeners know that this is the month when strawberries are at their best and in great demand at many of the events mentioned.

Midsummer Day should be 21st June: that day in the year when the northern half of the earth is nearest the sun and therefore has most daylight hours. However, the feast of St. John the Baptist is on 24th June, and although the "longest day" is past, the later date has wrongly become known as Midsummer Day. For many centuries this was one of the most popular holidays of the year.

July: 31 days

July is our seventh month. The Romans called it *Quintilis*, the fifth month, but after the death of **Julius Caesar** they renamed it in his honour. He was born on 12th July 102 B.C. Until about two centuries ago it was pronounced "*Ju*ly", with the stress on the first syllable, as in *Ju*lius, but we now say "Ju*ly*".

The British weather in July has never been reliable. A proverb of 1732 runs:

> *"If the first of July be rainy weather,*
> *'Twill rain more or less for four weeks together."*

A similar saying refers to **St Swithin's Day** on 15th July:

> *"St Swithin's Day, if thou dost rain,*
> *For forty days it will remain.*
> *St Swithin's day, if thou be fair,*
> *For forty days 'twill rain no more."*

When it does rain on 15th July, country people say that St Swithin is "christening the apples". However, July can be very hot. John Clare calls it a month of "sultry days and dewy nights".

On the Isle of Man the **Tynwald** ceremony is held on 5th July on Tynwald Hill, St Johns. In the presence of the most important officials of the island, including the twenty-four members of the House of Keys, the world's smallest parliament, the Chief Justice reads aloud the titles of the Acts of Parliament which have been passed by the British parliament at Westminster during the year. He reads them first in English, then in Manx, the old language of the Isle of Man. A ceremony of reading out the laws made during the year goes back to the tenth century, when the island was ruled by the Vikings.

On 4th July 1775 the American colonists declared themselves independent of Britain, and Americans still celebrate **Independence Day** on 4th July.

In France 14th July is **Bastille Day**, a public holiday celebrating the fall of the Bastille, a hated and feared prison fortress in Paris, in 1789.

20th July may turn out to be one of the most important dates in our future history books. On that day in 1969 a man stood on the moon for the first time. He was the American astronaut Neil Armstrong. As he stepped from the lunar module he said:

"That's one small step for man — a giant leap for mankind."

There was an old woman tossed up in a basket,
Seventeen times as high as the moon;
And where she was going, I couldn't but ask it,
For in her hand she carried a broom.
Old woman, old woman, old woman, quoth I,
O whither, O whither, O whither so high?
To sweep the cobwebs off the sky!
Shall I go with you? Aye, by-and-by.

49

August: 31 days

August is our eighth month. The Romans called it *Sextilis*, the sixth month, since their year started with March. They later renamed it after **Augustus**, their first emperor.

The Saxons called it *weod monath*, the month of weeds.

August can be a month of very warm weather. Under the First French Republic part of August was called *thermidor*, the month of heat.

In Britain this is the peak holiday month, when all schools are closed. In France many businesses and shops also close down, as the owners are away on holiday. In Germany school summer holidays are staggered, from state to state, so that children in Bavaria, for example, may end their summer term in early July, while children in Lower Saxony may end theirs in early August. The following year the rota is changed.

The **Royal National Eisteddfod of Wales** is usually held in the first week of August. An *eisteddfod* means a 'sitting', and the first recorded contest of poets and musicians was held in 1176 in Cardigan Castle. Nowadays there are competitions for choral and orchestral works, drama, poetry, brass band music, and many other activities. As it is a "national" eisteddfod, the official language is naturally Welsh; an international version is held in July, when many languages can be heard.

In Britain **The Glorious Twelfth** is important to some people. From 12th August the shooting of grouse is officially permitted, and those who take part in this activity often travel to Scotland or grouse moors elsewhere to start the first day of the shooting season with a bang.

15th August is the religious festival of the **Assumption of the Blessed Virgin Mary** and is thought to be the day when she was taken up bodily into Heaven at the end of her earthly life. This is a public holiday in many Roman Catholic countries, and is often celebrated with special masses and colourful processions in honour of Mary. In Spain bullfights are frequently part of the *fiesta*.

In mid-August the Royal International Horse Show is held in Wembley Arena, and throughout the month cricket is played and watched by thousands on village greens and county grounds in all parts of the country.

The Late Summer Bank Holiday — once called the August Bank Holiday — is now on the last Monday in August. For many people it used to mean a trip to the seaside. Dylan Thomas describes such an occasion in his piece for radio entitled *Holiday Memory*. "August Bank Holiday. A tune on an ice-cream cornet. A slap of sea and a tickle of sand. A fanfare of sunshades opening. A tuck of dresses. A rolling of trousers. A sunburn of girls and a lark of boys ... In those always radiant, rainless, lazily rowdy and sky-blue summers departed, I remember August Monday..."

Laurie Lee recalls similar carefree days in a Gloucestershire village in *Cider with Rosie*. "Summer was also the time ... of butter running like oil, of sunstroke, fever and cucumber peel stuck cool to one's burning brow. All this, and the feeling that it would never end, that such days had come for ever, with the pump drying up and the water-butt crawling, and the chalk ground hard as the moon. All sights twice-brilliant and smells twice-sharp, all game-days twice as long..."

In the small Derbyshire town of Eyam, the last Sunday in August is known as **Plague Sunday**. This recalls the most important time in the town's history. In 1665 a box of infected cloth was sent from London, where the plague had broken out, to the village tailor in Eyam. The plague now appeared in Eyam and threatened to spread throughout Derbyshire and further afield. The people of Eyam, led by their rector, William Mompesson, heroically decided to contain the plague within their community, so that the disease should not spread. The church was closed, but services were held in the open air in Cucklet Dell; the people of neighbouring villages left food at a boundary of the village for the Eyam people to collect. Their isolation lasted thirteen months, and during that time 259 of the 350 villagers died, including William Mompesson's wife. On Plague Sunday a memorial service is always held in Cucklet Dell.

September: 30 days

This is our ninth month. It was the seventh month of the Roman year and gets its name from the Latin word *septem*, seven. The Saxons called it *haerfest monath* or harvest month.

It is still a time of intense activity for all farmers until the harvest is safely gathered in. Flora Thompson describes a typical harvest scene in her *Lark Rise to Candleford*:

"...the last load was brought in, with a nest of merry boys' faces among the sheaves on the top, and the men walking alongside with pitchforks on shoulders. As they passed along the roads they shouted:

'Harvest home! Harvest home!
Merry, merry, merry harvest home!'

and women came to their cottage gates and waved ... and the farmer came out, followed by his daughters and maids with jugs and bottles and mugs, and drinks were handed round amidst general congratulations. Then the farmer invited the men to his harvest home dinner..."

Flora Thompson then goes on to describe in detail a lively harvest supper enjoyed by the whole village. John Clare's

Northamptonshire countrymen also made the most of the annual festivity:

> *"Then comes the harvest supper night*
> *Which rustics welcome with delight,*
> *When merry game and tiresome tale*
> *And songs increasing with the ale*
> *Their mingled uproar interpose*
> *To crown the harvest's happy close,*
> *While rural mirth that there abides*
> *Laughs till she almost cracks her sides."*

These days many churches and chapels, in country and town, hold harvest festivals as services of thanksgiving for the harvest and other blessings.

Fairs often take place at this time of year: part fun-fair, part cattle market. The Germans call such a market *Stoppelmarkt*, "stubble market", because it is held when the crops have been harvested and only the stubble remains. In this country many "mop fairs" take place (e.g. at Tewkesbury, Warwick and Stratford). These gatherings were originally "job centres", where servants and farm workers could seek new employment. In Thomas Hardy's novel *Far from the Madding Crowd* there is a description of such a fair at Casterbridge: "Carters and waggoners were distinguished by having a piece of whip-cord twisted round their hats, thatchers wore a fragment of woven straw; shepherds held their sheep-crooks in their hands; and thus the situation required was known to the hirers at a glance." Servant girls would carry a mop, and so we get the name for these hiring fairs.

The first Monday in September is **Labor Day** in North America. Trade unions hold public meetings, parades and street fairs.

1st September, 1971, is a date which may be remembered rather regretfully by your parents. This was the day on which decimalization of our currency officially began. After this, the days of the sixpence, the threepenny bit, the half crown and the ha'penny were numbered.

For children of school age — and their parents — early September means the beginning of another school year. For the youngest children it marks the start of eleven years of compulsory education. In Germany these beginners are given a *Schultüte*, a "school bag", to help them through the first anxious hours. It is a large cone of shiny or decorated cardboard filled with sweets, fruit and small treats; sometimes it is nearly as tall as the little owner. Often a photographer is at hand to record the day for the proud parents.

Laurie Lee also recorded his first day at school. It began like this: "The morning came, without any warning, when my sisters surrounded me, wrapped me in scarves, tied up my bootlaces, thrust a cap on my head, and stuffed a baked potato in my pocket.

"'What's this?' I said.

'You're starting school today.'

'I ain't. I'm stopping 'ome.'"

But he wasn't; and you can read more of what happened on that day in his book *Cider with Rosie*.

In "soft September" fruit-pickers are at their busiest. An old saying runs hopefully, "September blow soft till fruit be in loft". Gradually we notice the nip of autumn in the air; leaves begin to fall and we remember that the North American name for autumn is "The Fall".

29th September is the feast of St Michael the Archangel, a day known for centuries as **Michaelmas.** It was one of the four "quarter-days", days on which, by tradition, rent had to be paid. (The other three quarter-days were Lady Day (25th March), Midsummer (24th June) and Christmas (25th December). Michael was at one time one of the most popular of the saints. Many churches have been dedicated to this "prince of the heavenly host". Often these churches are on hilltops (perhaps because they were thought to be nearer to heaven), for example the now ruined churches on Brent Tor in Devon and Glastonbury Tor in Somerset. Even better known are St. Michael's Mount off the Cornish coast, and Mont St Michel off the coast of Normandy.

St Michael's Mount

A "Michaelmas goose" was a traditional delicacy at this time of year when geese were at their best, and Michaelmas daisies are autumn flowers.

Music-lovers look forward to a very "English" occasion which usually takes place in September: the Last Night of the Proms. For eighty-eight seasons the Henry Wood Promenade Concerts have been taking place in the Albert Hall in London. The last night is always a colourful cheerful occasion, usually shown on television.

October: 31 days

This was the Romans' eighth month. Its name comes from *octo*, the Latin word for eight.

The poet John Clare, writing in his *Shepherd's Calendar*, says of October:

> *"Nature now spreads around in dreary hue*
> *A pall to cover all that summer knew..."*

It can be a wet, cold and rather dismal month for us in Britain, though in Zimbabwe people are sweltering in intense heat before the rains begin, and they call October "suicide month". T. S. Eliot saw a different side to it when he called the month "golden October", because leaves turn gold before they fall. The Saxons called it *win monath*: wine month — because the grapes are ripe and wine is made from them. Today you can buy a German wine called *goldener Oktober*. In Munich, South Germany, the *Oktoberfest*, coinciding with the wine harvest, is held in this month. It is a time for enjoying oneself — and an excuse for drinking a great deal of beer.

In early October the three-day **Nottingham Goose Fair** takes place. It was granted a charter in 1284 by Edward I. Today it is solely a fun fair, but in the Middle Ages as many as 20,000 geese were offered for sale. They had been driven there during the previous weeks in great flocks from Lincolnshire and Norfolk.

'Bobbing for apples'

The last day of October is **Hallowe'en**, the eve of All Hallows' or All Saints' Day. The Celts celebrated their New Year's Eve on this night. Because they believed that spirits were abroad, they built bonfires to frighten them away, and feasted and danced round the fires. We still build bonfires and celebrate with feasting at this time of year, but nowadays usually on 5th November, **Bonfire Night**. Nevertheless, the origins of these celebrations lie back in pagan times, when the evil spirits of darkness had to be driven away with noise and fire.

The so-called **October Revolution** took place in Russia in 1917 under the leadership of Lenin. The old way of life was overthrown, the members of the Russian royal family were executed, and eventually the U.S.S.R. (the Union of Soviet Socialist Republics) was formed.

The Hindu feast of **Dussehra** takes place at this time of year. It is followed about three weeks later by **Diwali**, the Hindu New Year, so the whole festival season lasts nearly a month. The most important feature of the celebrations is a cycle of plays based on the events in the life of Rama, a prince, and Sita, his wife. There are so many adventures in this *Ramayana* that the whole cycle of plays can take up to a month of evening performances. The villain of the piece is the ten-headed, ten-armed demon king, Ravana, who is eventually outwitted.

On the last night of Dussehra a huge effigy of Ravana is set up in the open, then burnt. Firecrackers inside the figure explode and Ravana's wickedness comes to a spectacular end.

In readiness for Diwali, the Hindu "Festival of Lights" and the New Year, homes are cleaned thoroughly and "deepa" or "diva" — tiny lights — are lighted and set in the windows. The preparations are said to commemorate the coronation of Sita and Rama; the thousands of tiny lights will guide them home after their adventures. Lakshmi, the goddess of prosperity, will also visit homes that are full of light, and bring them good fortune in the coming year.

November: 30 days

This is our eleventh month, but it was the ninth of the Roman year, so it gets its name from the Latin word for nine: *novem.*

Few people find November very pleasant. The Saxons called it *blut-monath*: blood month, because animals were slaughtered before the onset of winter. The poet T. S. Eliot called it "Sombre November". Sir Walter Scott, in his long poem *Marmion*, wrote in 1808:

> *"November's sky is chill and drear,*
> *November's leaf is red and sear (withered)."*

John Clare in *The Shepherd's Calendar* observed:

> *"Thus wears the month along in chequered moods:*
> *Sunshine and shadow, tempest loud and calms;*
> *One hour dies silent o'er the sleepy woods,*
> *The next wakes loud with unexpected storms."*

Another poet, Thomas Hood, tried to sum up all his dislike of the month when he wrote:

> "No *warmth*, no *cheerfulness*, no *healthful ease*,
> No *comfortable feel in any member* —
> No *shade*, no *shine*, no *butterflies*, no *bees*,
> No *fruits*, no *flowers*, no *leaves*, no *birds*, —
> *November!*"

Here is another sour warning to bear in mind:

> "*Ice in November enough to bear a duck,*
> *All the coming winter will be mud and muck.*"

Yet November, for all its dreariness, is the time of several colourful events. 1st November is the feast of **All Saints** or **All Hallows**, as it used to be called. On this day Christians remember all "men of good will", great ones and forgotten ones, who have died through the ages.

5th November is **Bonfire Night**. It is also called **Guy Fawkes Night**, after a soldier, Guy Fawkes, who with other conspirators plotted to blow up the King, his son, and members of both Houses of Parliament in 1605. Luckily the plot was discovered in time, so the following year the government ruled that 5th November should from then on be "a day of thanksgiving".

Just as in 1605, a new session of Parliament in London is still opened by the reigning monarch at the beginning of November.

11th November is **Remembrance Day**, when those who have died in war are remembered, and the same date is called **Veterans' Day** in North America. On this day those who have served their country in the armed forces are remembered.

The **Lord Mayor's Show** takes place in London on the second Saturday in November, to mark the start of the new Lord Mayor of London's year of office.

The fourth Thursday in November is **Thanksgiving Day** in the U.S.A. It recalls the Pilgrim Fathers' harvest of 1621, their first after they landed in America.

22nd November is **St Cecilia's Day**. She is thought to have been a Roman maiden who was martyred in the second or third century. Her story is told in the "Second Nun's Tale" in Chaucer's *Canterbury Tales*. She was adopted as patroness of the Academy of Music in Rome in 1584, and the famous artist Raphael painted a picture of her. She is usually portrayed at the organ, and is the patron saint of musicians.

The poet W. H. Auden wrote an *Anthem for St Cecilia's Day*. It was dedicated to the composer Benjamin Britten, who set it to music in 1942. It describes how "this holy lady ... poured forth her song in perfect calm". The poet then begs her:

> *"Blessed Cecilia, appear in visions*
> *to all musicians, appear and inspire ..."*

Concerts and recitals are often given on St Cecilia's Day.

December: 31 days

This is the twelfth and last month. Its name comes from the Latin word *decem*, meaning ten, since it was the tenth month in the Roman year. The Saxons called it *winter monath*, winter month, but after many of them became Christian, they renamed it *heligh monath* or holy month, because Christmas, the birth of Jesus, is celebrated in December.

At the beginning of December, the season of **Advent** starts. The word "advent" means "coming", and as its name suggests, it is a time of preparation for the coming feast of Christmas. Children enjoy hanging up an Advent calendar, either bought or home-made, and opening one of its little cardboard doors each morning to reveal the seasonal picture inside. On 24th December, Christmas Eve, the scene is always of the baby Jesus lying in the stable at Bethlehem.

6th December is the feast day of **St Nicholas**, who was very highly regarded in past centuries, as you can judge from the thousands of old churches dedicated to him. Nicholas was a bishop in the fourth century, and is the patron saint of Russia, of children, and of pawnbrokers, so he has a wide appeal. There are many legends about him.

He is often shown in pictures standing next to three children in a tub. It is said that they had been killed and pickled in a famine and given to Nicholas as food. He miraculously brought them back to life.

In other pictures (as in the one in the National Gallery of Scotland by the artist Jacques Louis David) he is shown giving gifts of money as dowries to the three daughters of a poor man. It is said that the three bags of gold are the origin of the three gold balls, which is the sign hanging above pawnbrokers' shops.

According to the legend, Nicholas left the money while the girls were asleep, and so began the pleasant custom of giving gifts in secret on his feast day, which was gradually transferred to Christmas. In Holland St Nicholas is "San Nicolaas" and when Dutch colonists took the name to America it changed to Santa Claus.

At one time it was the custom, both on the Continent and in this country, to appoint a boy bishop in churches and cathedrals on 6th December. He was dressed in bishop's robes and allowed certain privileges, including preaching from the pulpit. His "reign" ended on 28th December, Holy Innocents' Day.

13th December is **St Lucia's Day**, a special day in Sweden, where it is a festival of light (Lucia means "light"). The day starts fairly early with a charming custom: the eldest daughter of the family, dressed in white, wearing a crown of pine twigs decorated with lighted candles, brings her parents coffee in bed! Later she sits in a place of honour at the family breakfast table in a brilliantly lit room. The feast day even extends to schools, which are particularly brightly lit for the occasion.

24th December is **Christmas Eve**, children's favourite night of the year. British children hang up a stocking, sock or pillow-case, knowing that Father Christmas will stop his reindeer, come down the chimney and fill the stocking with good things.

It is a tradition that Jesus was born at midnight and many Christian services start at that time in honour of Christ's birthday on **Christmas Day,** 25th December. Every family, town and nation has its own traditional ways of celebrating this joyful feast, but some customs are common to all: decorating the house in some way beforehand, singing carols, exchanging cards and gifts, making or putting out a model crib scene to represent the stable at Bethlehem, and eating particularly seasonal foods.

However, there had been celebrations (by sun-worshippers) at this time of year long before Christianity. The Romans too celebrated a feast called the **Saturnalia,** in honour of the god Saturn (see page 89), which lasted some days. The festivities included much feasting and merrymaking, with bonfires and torchlight. The sun was welcomed back after the shortest day, the winter solstice, on 21st December. In its honour 25th December was dedicated to the birthday of the unconquered sun: *Dies Natalis Invicti Solis.*

Later, in Scandinavian countries, Yule logs were burnt in honour of their greatest gods, Odin and Thor. **Yule** or Jul, was the ancient name of the Thor festival, and is still the Swedish name for Christmas.

Some people have even suggested that legends about Odin, or Woden as he was called by the Anglo-Saxons (see page 82), led to some of our stories about Father Christmas. Odin, wearing a long cloak and a wide hat, was said to lash his eight-legged horse, Sleipnir, across the skies, just as Father Christmas in cloak and hood is thought to drive his reindeer.

26th December is "the feast of Stephen", the first Christian martyr. It is also traditionally known as **Boxing Day.** On this day, church poor boxes were opened and the alms money shared out among the poor of the parish. Later, it was the custom to give servants a Christmas bonus, which they came to expect. John Clare describes how:

"The prentice boy wi' ruddy face
And rime bepowdered dancing locks
From door to door wi' happy pace
Runs round to claim his 'Christmas box'."

28th December is the **Day of the Holy Innocents**, recalling the babies killed by Herod in his search for the baby Jesus.

In Spain this is the equivalent of our April Fool's Day. Instead of calling someone an April Fool, you call them an *innocente* (someone who is naive or simple), and try to play jokes on them or send them on fruitless errands. It has been suggested that there is a connection here with Herod's unsuccessful search for Jesus among the "innocents".

31st December is the last day of the year or, more optimistically, **New Year's Eve**. Many people see the old year out with a party, welcoming in the New Year with toasts of champagne, and exchanging good wishes for a "Happy New Year". This celebration is particularly dear to the Scots. They call it **Hogmanay** and welcome in the New Year with much spirit.

In Yorkshire, those who are wide enough awake to remember say "Black rabbits, black rabbits, black rabbits" in the closing seconds of the old year. Then they say, "White rabbits, white rabbits, white rabbits," as their first utterance of the New Year. This is supposed to bring luck.

Many children try to make "White rabbits, white rabbits, white rabbits" their first words on the first day of any new month. When they get to school they may say to someone:

"A pinch, a punch, the first of the month — and no returns!"

In retaliation the other one will immediately exclaim:

"A punch and a kick for being so quick — and no returns!"

To which there really seems no answer.

⤜ THE ZODIAC ⤛

The **Babylonians** who lived in what is now Iraq built huge temples as long ago as 3000 B.C. From those temples they worshipped their gods – the sun, the moon and the planet Venus – and observed the skies. They gave names to certain groups of stars or constellations which could be seen only at a certain time of the year.

The Romans later gave the constellations Roman names, and named the planets (apart from Earth) after their gods and goddesses. They believed that the planets and constellations had power over people's lives, and that their good fortune in life depended on the position of the planets in the sky.

The study of the stars and planets is called **astronomy**, but the study of their effect on a person's life is called **astrology**. Until a few centuries ago astrology was taken very seriously, and people would go to an "astrologer" and pay him to cast their "horoscope" – to forecast their future according to the stars. There was even a Royal Astrologer attached to many royal households, who would work out the most favourable time for the king to wage war, make peace or marry.

Many magazines and newspapers today still publish horoscopes, and people like to look up their own prospects for the week under their own "sign of the zodiac", though the predictions are so vague that they could apply to anyone.

The word "zodiac" comes from the Greek words which mean "animal circle", because the Greeks and Romans gave animal names to so many of the twelve constellations which seem to form a circle in the night sky. Astrologers still use the Latin names, and connect each constellation with certain days:

Aries (ram): 21st March–20th April
Taurus (bull): 21st April–20th May
Gemini (twins): 21st May–20th June
Cancer (crab): 21st June–21st July
Leo (lion): 22nd July–21st August
Virgo (virgin): 22nd August–21st September
Libra (scales): 22nd September–22nd October
Scorpio (scorpion): 23rd October–21st November
Sagittarius (archer): 22nd November–20th December
Capricorn (goat): 21st December–19th January
Aquarius (water-carrier): 20th January–18th February
Pisces (fish): 19th February–20th March

☙ THE JEWISH YEAR ☙

Jews now normally follow the Gregorian calendar, like the majority of peoples in the world, but they also keep their own religious calendar. This is measured in lunar months, and dates back to the beginnings of their history. The Jewish year 5745 A.M. begins on 27 September 1984. A.M. stands for *anno mundi*, which means "year of the world".

The twelve lunar months in the Jewish year have alternately thirty and twenty-nine days, so they do not correspond exactly with the months in the Gregorian calendar. All Jewish months begin at a new moon, and a thirteenth "leap month" is added seven times in a cycle of nineteen years.

Here is a list of the Jewish months with some important dates:

1. *Tishri* (Sept.–Oct.)
   1st: Rosh Hashanah, the Jewish New Year.
   10th: Yom Kippur, the Day of Atonement, a time of repentance.
   15th: Sukkot, the Feast of Tabernacles, which lasts a week, originally, and still observed as, a Harvest Festival.
2. *Marcheshvan* (Oct.–Nov.)
3. *Kislev* (Nov.–Dec.)
   25th: Hanukah, the Festival of Lights, lasting eight days. It commemorates the re-dedication of the Temple in Jerusalem in 165 B.C. (after Antiochus IV had made it

unholy by placing an idol there) and the miraculous flow of oil with which the Temple lamp was kept alight for eight days.

4. *Tevet* (Dec.–Jan.)
5. *Shevat* (Jan.–Feb.)
6. *Adar* (Feb.–March)

   14th: Purim. This commemorates the deliverance of the Jews of Persia, as told in the Biblical Book of Esther.

   (The "leap" month Adar Sheni, *or* Ve-Adar, is added here.)
7. *Nisan* (March–April)

   14th–22nd: Pesach or Passover (see page 41). This commemorates the deliverance of the Hebrews (Jews) from the Egypt of the Pharaohs; you can read in the Biblical book of Exodus about how the angel of the Lord "passed over" the homes of the Jews while punishing the Egyptians.
8. *Iyyar* (April–May)
9. *Sivan* (May–June)

   6th: Shavuot, or Pentecost, always occurs fifty days after Passover. It commemorates the giving of the Pentateuch (the first five books of the Old Testament) to Moses on Mount Sinai.
10. *Tamuz* (June–July)
11. *Av* (July–Aug.)
12. *Elul* (Aug.–Sept.)

The Jewish week starts on a Sunday and the days are known as the first day of the week, the second day of the week, etc., until Sabbath Eve (Friday) and the Sabbath (Saturday).

The day of twenty-four hours runs from sunset to sunset, as the first evening came before the morning, according to the Biblical story of the Creation in the Book of Genesis.

CESTHE MUSLIM YEAR CSO

The eight hundred million Muslims throughout the world are followers of their Holy Prophet, Muhammad. Their religion is called Islam. The Islamic calendar is lunar, each month beginning with a new moon. For this reason, the twelve months in their religious year do not coincide with those in the Gregorian calendar. The Islamic months are:

1. Muharram (1st day of Muharram is New Year's Day)
2. Safar
3. Rabi I
4. Rabi II
5. Jamadi I
6. Jamadi II
7. Rajab
8. Shaban
9. Ramadan (the fasting month)
10. Shaval
11. Ziqad
12. Zil-Haj

The ninth month is the most important. Its name, **Ramadan**, means "restoring", and throughout this month Muslims try to restore their spiritual life. They do this by taking no food and drink – not even water – between sunrise and sunset, and by saying special prayers and reading their Holy Book, the Qur'an or Koran, with special devotion. Eating and drinking and even

70

entertainments are allowed between sunset and sunrise during Ramadan, so in Muslim countries people sleep during the day when they can, and enjoy public performances such as shadow plays which are put on during the night.

Ramadan ends with sunrise on the first day of the tenth month. This is the first day of Eid (or Id)-al-Fitr, the festival of breaking the fast; it lasts three or four days and is a time of thanksgiving and rejoicing. The first day of the Eid begins with a special prayer at sunrise, then a bath and clean or new clothes. An essential part of the festival is the "fitra", the giving of money to poorer people. It is the custom to visit relatives and friends, enjoying one another's hospitality. For children this is a time of cards, gifts and parties, rather like Christmas.

On the first day of the Eid there are also vast congregational gatherings, where all present prostrate themselves before Allah, offering thanks and glorifying him. In a Karachi newspaper on the Eid-al-fitr of the Muslim year 1402 AH (22nd July, 1982) there was this typical announcement:

> *"Eid Prayer at the National Stadium ...*
> *Eid Prayer will be held at 8.30 a.m. sharp."*

(The "hejira" or 'hijra' marks the beginning of the Muslim calendar. You can read more about it on page 99.

The second great festival of the Islamic year is Eid-al-Adha. It is called the "sacrificial festival" and is connected with "haj" or pilgrimage to Mecca. There is community worship, often in some open place, to mark the start of the festival. There is a special meal, something like a "Christmas dinner". The animals have been slaughtered according to the proper ritual; the families cook and eat a third of the meat immediately and the remaining two-thirds are given to relatives or poorer people. As at Eid-al-fitr new clothes are worn, gifts and greetings are exchanged, and rich foods are eaten.

Friday is the holy day of the Muslim week (see page 88).

⊂⊄ THE WEEK ⊃⊅

We saw in "The Calendar" (page 11) that the length of a year depends on the earth's movement round the sun, and the length of a month on the moon's movement round the earth. A week is quite different; it is a man-made division of time, and there is no rule about its length. The word "week" comes from a much older word which meant "turn" or "change". Different peoples have divided up the month in different ways, although the seven-day week is the commonest nowadays.

The **Ancient Egyptians,** for instance, divided their months of thirty days into three weeks of ten days each; so did the heads of the short-lived **First French Republic** in 1793. They called their week a *décade*, that is, something with ten parts. At one time in **Scandinavia** a week was a group of five days only. The **Jews** always had a seven-day week, according to the account at the beginning of the Bible. There you can read about the creation of the world, and how: "By the seventh day God had come to an end of making, and rested..."

The **Romans** first divided up the month according to a system of their own, but later they began to use the seven-day week like the Jews. They called the seven days after the sun, the moon, and the planets Mars, Mercury, Jupiter, Venus and Saturn. The planets themselves were – and still are – called after the gods whom the Romans had worshipped before they became Christians.

If you look at the table on page 74 you will see that versions of the Roman names for the days of the week are still used in many European countries, as they have been since the fourth century A.D. This is because these countries were part of the Roman Empire, and their languages are derived from Latin, the language of the Romans (for this reason they are sometimes called Romance languages). The modern, artificial language

Esperanto was made up by using parts of various Romance languages.

The languages of Northern Europe were not derived from Latin (even though Britain was part of the Roman Empire for a time). Their names for the days Tuesday–Friday come from the names of northern gods and goddesses who correspond to the Latin ones. For instance, "Friday" comes from the name of Frigga, the northern goddess of love, whereas the French for "Friday" is *vendredi*, meaning the day of Venus, the Roman goddess of love.

All civilized communities now have a seven-day week. This has become a necessity, so that transport timetables and other communications can be understood all over the world. (However, some schools prefer to run on a "6-day week" or an "8-day week". The children soon get used to this timetable, and remember which lessons and homework to expect on a particular day. Day 7 may be Monday, Tuesday or any other weekday, but on their school timetable it will always follow Day 6 and be followed by Day 8.)

The "official" day of international timetables is the twenty-four-hour period from one midnight to the next. This is the **civic day.** But "day" can also mean the hours of natural light between dawn and sunset, and this is the **natural day.**

At the Equator there are equal periods of twelve hours' light and darkness every day of the year, but in most countries the "natural" day is of a slightly different length every twenty-four hours, as the earth is tilted slightly nearer the sun or slightly away from the sun. In the northern hemisphere the longest day comes in June (see page 12).

In this country the hours of daylight are calculated in advance and are published in newspapers and almanacs. Evening papers usually print the "lighting-up time", to remind drivers when to switch on their lights.

The Names of the Days of the Week in Different Languages

English	Norwegian	German	Latin
Sunday	søndag	Sonntag	solis dies
Monday	mandag	Montag	lunae dies
Tuesday	tirsdag	Dienstag	Martis dies
Wednesday	onsdag	Mittwoch	Mercurii dies
Thursday	torsdag	Donnerstag	Jovis dies
Friday	fredag	Freitag	Veneris dies
Saturday	lørdag	Sonnabend/ Samstag	Saturni dies

French	Spanish	Italian	Welsh
dimanche	domingo	domenica	dydd Sul
lundi	lunes	lunedì	dydd Llun
mardi	martes	martedì	dydd Mawrth
mercredi	miércoles	mercoledì	dydd Mercher
jeudi	jueves	giovedì	dydd Iau
vendredi	viernes	venerdì	dydd Gwener
samedi	sábado	sabato	dydd Sadwrn

Esperanto	Jewish	
dimanĉo	the first day of the week	⎫
lundo	the second day of the week	⎪
mardo	the third day of the week	names
merkredo	the fourth day of the week	translated
ĵaŭdo	the fifth day of the week	from
vendredo	Sabbath Eve	the Hebrew
sabato	the Sabbath Day	⎭

First French Republic
primidi, duodi, tridi, quartidi, quintidi, sextidi, septidi, octidi, nonidi, décadi

74

Sunday

In most early religions the **sun** was worshipped as a god. The Egyptians called him **Ra,** the creator. The Inca rulers of Peru regarded him as the chief of the gods and the Inca priests wore vestments decorated with a sunflower made of real gold.

The Greeks called him **Helios,** or **Apollo.** The Romans also believed in the god Apollo and honoured him with the title "Sol, the Unconquerable One". They called the first day of the week after him: *solis dies* or Sun-day. They thought that he rose at dawn and drove a fiery chariot across the sky, sinking out of sight at dusk. In the British Museum in London there is a silver-gilt disc showing the sun god with rays of light shining from his head, and four horses ready to speed with his chariot on his daily journey.

There is a story of Clytia, an ocean nymph, who wasted away for love of Helios, the sun-god. She changed into a lilac-coloured, sweet-smelling flower which still bears his name:

heliotrope. This flower, like other 'heliotropic' plants, still shows its devotion to the sun by turning towards it throughout the day.

In his poem "Flowers" Thomas Hood calls the heliotrope: "the mad Clytia whose head is turned by the sun." Another Greek legend tells of how Helios one day allowed his son, Phæthon, to drive the sun-chariot. The horses raced out of control, blazing a streak across the heavens, which became the Milky Way. Then they plunged down and scorched the earth; Zeus later sent a flood to cool it down after this disaster.

One of the Seven Wonders of the World was the Colossus of Rhodes, a huge statue of Helios, wearing a crown with rays, at the entrance to Rhodes Harbour.

The once famous city of Heliopolis was called after the sun god; the modern city of Cairo in Egypt has grown up near the site of ancient Heliopolis.

The Jews made the seventh day of the week a day of rest, which they called the Sabbath. The Christians kept the idea of a holy day, but chose Sunday, because this was the day when Christ rose from the dead. (The Russian word for Sunday, *Voskreseniye*, means "resurrection".) In the Romance languages the word for Sunday is connected with the Latin word *dominus*, meaning "lord". The Greek name for Sunday is *kuriaki*, which means "of the Lord". Sunday is the Lord's Day.

76

Constantine, the first Roman Emperor to become a Christian, decreed that all work except essential farm work should stop on Sunday, and in Christian countries Sunday has been a holiday for most people ever since, though there are now other forms of essential work that have to be continued on Sunday.

Some later Christians took their observance of the day of rest to ridiculous lengths, forbidding any innocent and lively activities that might have made the day more enjoyable. One seventeenth-century writer gave a sarcastic description of this kind of person:

> *"Hanging of his cat on Monday*
> *For killing of a mouse on Sunday."*

When Sunday schools for children who worked in factories during the week were started in 1780 by Robert Raikes of Gloucester, some people disapproved of the idea, in case they interfered with the children's "Sunday observance", and their religious duties were neglected. In fact, it was only through the Sunday schools that thousands of these children received any education of any sort. After labouring down the pit or in the mill for up to twelve hours a day they often fell asleep at Sunday school, so their "Sunday observance" would not have been very attentive in any case.

In the later nineteenth century Sunday in Britain became even stricter and duller, and instead of being enjoyed, it was dreaded, particularly by children in well brought-up families, for whom Sunday school had now become acceptable. The children were expected to go to church twice and to Sunday school in between. They were not allowed to read a book, play with toys or have games outside. One little boy said that the only form of amusement permitted to him was looking through the family photograph album.

Nowadays, Sunday is a "day of rest", when most people are able to take it easy and relax from the paid work of the other five or six days. Sunday dinner or Sunday lunch is still the main meal of the week in many households, and provides the best opportunity for eating as a family (even though this is not much of a rest for the one who does the cooking!). Christians still go to church to worship and keep Sunday as the Lord's Day in commemoration of Christ's resurrection on "the first day of the week", and Easter itself is always kept on a Sunday.

On the mainland of Europe there is a carefree and relaxed attitude to Sunday. Cafés and restaurants are open, so are many shops; football matches, dances and other amusements take place regularly. In Britain we are very cautiously trying to make Sunday less dull and more enjoyable and interesting. However, narrow tradition lingers on: for instance, there is still very little sport on Sunday, apart from some cricket, and very little entertainment, unless one lives in a large city. In London, for instance, the Petticoat Lane market is now a colourful Sunday tradition.

A child born on Sunday is supposed to be specially blessed.

> *"The child of Sunday and Christmas Day*
> *Is good and fair, and wise and gay."*

It has always been considered lucky to undertake something on a Sunday, for "the better the day, the better the deed". Perhaps a writer in the *Spectator* nearly three hundred years ago most neatly summed up the best side of Sunday, when he said that it "clears away the rust of the whole week".

> For birthdays:
> *Monday's child is fair of face,*
> *Tuesday's child is full of grace,*
> *Wednesday's child is full of woe,*
> *Thursday's child has far to go,*
> *Friday's child is loving and giving,*
> *Saturday's child works hard for his living;*
> *And the child that is born on the Sabbath day*
> *Is bonny and blithe and good and gay.*

78

Monday

This is the second day of the week, and it is called after the **moon,** as you can see in the English, Norwegian and German names given on page 74. The words for Monday in the Romance languages and also in Welsh and Esperanto come from *luna*, the Latin for "moon".

The Romans thought of the moon as Artemis or **Diana,** the sister of Apollo, the sun god. He drove his golden chariot across the sky each day, and then, as it sank from sight at sunset, Diana would set off, steering her silver chariot across the heavens through the night.

In the daytime Diana was thought to be a huntress, enjoying the chase through the woods, a quiverful of arrows slung over one shoulder. The poet Ben Jonson addressed her:

> *"Queen and huntress chaste and fair,*
> *Now the sun is laid asleep,*
> *Seated in thy silver chair,*
> *State in wonted manner keep."*

Monday is the first day of the working week (except for clergymen, who regard it as their "day off"). Most of us wake up feeling "Mondayish": reluctant to start the working routine again. "Rainy days and Mondays always get me down," sing The Carpenters. Schoolboys used to have a special name for the day when school began after a holiday: Black Monday. Poor Clive James describes in his *Unreliable Memoirs* how he had "Mondayitis every day of the week. As my mother dragged me down the front path, I would clutch my stomach, cross my eyes, stick out my tongue, cough, choke, scream and vomit simultaneously" – an extreme case.

When workmen "kept the feast of Saint Monday", they were excusing their absence from work because of the ill effects of getting drunk on Sunday! Perhaps it was a wise move for

Parliament in the nineteenth century to pass Bank Holiday Acts, which gave working people the right to certain Mondays as holidays: Easter Monday, Whit Monday and the first Monday in August. (The last two have been renamed "Spring Bank Holiday" and "Late Summer Bank Holiday" and are now celebrated on the last Monday in May and the last Monday in August.)

For the industrious housewife, however, virtue would bring its own reward, for: "They that wash on Monday, have all the week to dry" – but that was in the days before women went out to work!

They that wash on Monday
Have all the week to dry.
They that wash on Tuesday
Are not so much awry.
They that wash on Wednesday
Are not so much to blame.
They that wash on Thursday
Wash for shame.
They that wash on Friday
Wash in need.
They that wash on Saturday –
Oh, they're sluts indeed!

Tuesday

Tuesday is the third day of the week. The Romans called this day after **Mars,** the god of war, as you can see in some of the names for this day on page 74. (Mars is also honoured in the month of March, see page 33.) "Tuesday" comes from the name of **Tiw,** a Saxon war god, one of the sons of Odin, (whom the Saxons called Woden) and the goddess Frigga. One-handed Tiw was a favourite: a courageous young warrior and protector of the gods.

One of the best known stories about him is his struggle with Fenris the Wolf. This was a ferocious beast which was kept in Asgard, the land of the gods. Only Tiw was prepared to go near enough to feed him. Fenris grew and grew and became monstrous, and a menace to all the gods. Twice they tried to chain him down; twice he flexed his muscles and snapped his bonds easily.

Tiw asked for help from some dwarfs, and in their underground workshops they fashioned some magic cords. They were made from: the sound of a cat's footfall, the beard of a woman, the roots of a rock, the breath of a fish, the sinews of a bear, and the spittle of a bird. Fenris agreed to let the gods tie him down with these magic bonds, provided that one of them would put his hand in the wolf's mouth. Tiw agreed. Although the wolf struggled furiously, it was unable to break the magic cords – and in its frenzied efforts to free itself, it bit off Tiw's hand.

Various places are called after him. Three villages in Warwickshire are called Lower, Middle and Upper Tysoe. Tysoe means "Tiw's ridge", and the ridge is the two hundred-metre-high hill nearby. In Surrey there is Tuesley (Tiw's glade) and in Devon there is Twiscombe (Tiw's valley).

The best known Tuesday in the year is **Shrove Tuesday** or Pancake Day. This is the day before Lent begins on **Ash**

Wednesday (see pages 31 and 84). Wise shopkeepers are well stocked up with lemons, as they are considered the best accompaniment to the traditional Shrove Tuesday pancakes.

Otherwise, Tuesday seems to be a very insignificant day of the week – except in Spain, where Tuesday the thirteenth is an unlucky day. *En trece y martes no te cases ni te embarques* is the Spanish saying: "On Tuesday the thirteenth, don't get married or go on board ship."

For sneezing:
Sneeze on Monday, sneeze for danger,
Sneeze on Tuesday, kiss a stranger,
Sneeze on Wednesday, get a letter,
Sneeze on Thursday, something better,
Sneeze on Friday, sneeze for sorrow,
Sneeze on Saturday, see your sweetheart tomorrow.

Wednesday

This is the fourth day of the week, which the Germans call simply *Mittwoch* or "midweek". It always seems the longest schoolday of the week, so some teachers wryly call it "suicide day".

In English, Wednesday means the day of **Woden.** He was an important god for the Saxons and they liked to trace the ancestry of their kings back to him. There are legends that King Alfred the Great, and even (some say) Queen Elizabeth II, are descendants of this Saxon god!

He was honoured at Wednesbury (Woden's "burgh" or fortified place), and at Wednesfield, both in Staffordshire. In Kent there may have been a temple erected in his honour at Woodnesborough. The Wansdyke (Woden's Dyke) was a long fortification of high rampart and deep trench, built by the West

Saxons against attacking tribes. Parts of it can still be seen in Somerset and Wiltshire.

In the Norse myths, Odin (as the Norsemen called Woden) was served by two ravens which brought him news from all corners of the earth. When he needed to travel, he rose faster than the wind on his eight-legged horse, Sleipnir. Odin had only one eye; he gave the other in return for a drink from the well of wisdom.

A group of maidens called Valkyries performed a special task for him: whenever heroes fell in battle, the Valkyries ("choosers of the slain") sped to fetch their souls to feast with Odin and Frigga, his wife, in the great hall of Valhalla. You can imagine how the battle-loving Valkyries, carrying swords and shields, raced across the skies, if you listen to Wagner's stirring "Ride of the Valkyries".

The memory of many of these mythical characters is still alive today: in the North Sea there are gas fields named "Odin", "Frig" and "Sleipnir", and an oilfield named "Valhall". The support vessel from which dives were made to the Tudor warship the *Mary Rose* was also called "Sleipnir".

Other names for Wednesday in the Romance languages honour the Roman god **Mercury** (he was known to the Greeks as **Hermes**). He had wings on the heels of his sandals and a winged cap. He carried a magic staff which is usually shown entwined with ribbons or snakes. Like Woden, he had magical wisdom and guided the souls of the dead. Mercury was an eloquent speaker and the gods' messenger. You may know of a newspaper called the *Mercury*.

At some time you may have tried to touch a few drops of the element mercury, which is used in thermometers. It is bright and shining and moves so fast that it always escapes from your fingers. You can see why it is also known as "quicksilver". If someone is called "mercurial", it means that he has the gift of persuasive speech, is swift in thought and action, quick to change mood, and hard to pin down.

The most important Wednesday in the Christian year is **Ash Wednesday,** the first day of Lent, when the period of preparation for the great feast of Easter begins. For centuries ashes have been connected with penitence. In some Christian churches on this day the priest will mark a cross on the foreheads of the congregation, saying:

*"Remember, man, that thou art dust
And unto dust thou must return."*

The Irish have a special name for the Wednesday two days before Good Friday at the end of Lent: they call it **Spy Wednesday.** This refers to Judas, who spied on the movements of his friend Jesus, and later betrayed him.

For weddings:
*Monday for wealth, Tuesday for health,
Wednesday the best day of all;
Thursday for crosses, Friday for losses,
Saturday no luck at all.*

Thursday

This is the fifth day of the week, called in English after **Thor** or **Thunor,** one of the Northern gods. The German for Thursday, *Donnerstag,* means "Thunor's day". In Essex there is a place called Thundersley, and in Surrey there is Thursley; both these names mean "Thunor's glade". A temple was dedicated to him at Thundridge (Thunor's ridge) in Hertfordshire.

Thor was a god of growth and agriculture. He had red hair and was the strongest of the gods, known for being boastful and foolhardy. He was afraid of nothing. He wielded a hammer called Miolnir, and wore a pair of iron gauntlets and a magic belt which doubled his strength.

Some Giants once challenged him to undertake some apparently easy tasks. First they asked him to drain dry a drinking horn, but he was unable to. The more he drank, the more it filled, for the other end was in the sea. However, he caused the first ebb tide, and since then tides have ebbed and flowed in Thor's memory.

The Giants also asked him to lift up a large cat. He could barely move it, though in the end he lifted one paw. In reality the cat was the serpent which was coiled round the earth. Finally, he was challenged to wrestle with a frail old woman. She was amazingly strong and forced Thor to his knees. By this time, however, he had greatly impressed the Giants with his extraordinary strength, for the old woman was really Old Age, and every living person is finally overcome by her.

In the Romance languages Thursday is the day which honours **Jove** or **Jupiter**. Like Thor, he had connections with thunder: he hurled a thunderbolt as a weapon, and was known as "The Thunderer". If you visit excavated Roman army forts in Britain, you can still see altar stones with inscriptions in honour of "Jupiter the Best and Greatest". He was the mightiest of the gods on Mount Olympus, the gods' home, and the ruler of men on earth. The summits of mountains were sacred to him; the eagle was his special bird. He wore a wreath of oak or olive leaves, and bulls or goats were sacrificed to him. For centuries oaths have been sworn by his name: "By Jove!"

"Seven days
make one weak":

Solomon Grundy, born on a Monday,
Christened on Tuesday,
Married on Wednesday,
Very ill on Thursday,
Worse on Friday,
Died on Saturday,
Buried on Sunday;
This is the end of Solomon Grundy.

Friday

This is the sixth day of the week. In English and German we are reminded of **Frigga** (or **Frig** as she is also known), the wife of Odin. English places named after her include Froyle and Frobury (both meaning "Frig's hill") in Hampshire and Fryup ("Frig's marshy enclosure") in North Yorkshire. Friday is the only day named after a goddess, and is literally "lady's day", since the German word *Frau*, meaning "lady", "woman" or "Mrs", comes from Frigga's name.

She was the goddess of love, and the Romans also named Friday after their goddess of love: **Venus.** You can find remnants of her name in the words for "Friday" in the Romance languages and Welsh.

Frigga was the mother of Tiw and Thor (from whom we have the names of Tuesday and Thursday), but she had two other sons: Baldur the Beautiful and Hodur, his twin, who was born blind. One day Baldur sensed that he was soon to die, and he told his mother of his fears. Frigga couldn't bear to think that Baldur might soon be taken from her at the height of his youth and beauty. She forced a promise from all things on the earth – stones, metals, plants, beasts – that they would never harm her son. But Frigga forgot to ask the mistletoe plant.

A spiteful, mischief-making god called Loki discovered this and made an arrow from a mistletoe twig. He gave it to blind Hodur and whispered in his ear: "Aim it at Baldur, just for sport – you know all things have promised not to hurt him." Thinking it was part of a game, Hodur let Loki take his arm and point the arrow towards Baldur. Hodur let fly the arrow and the mistletoe twig pierced Baldur to the heart. He died immediately.

All the gods mourned, but none more than Frigga, his mother.

Friday is the day on which Jesus was crucified, and for centuries the Christian Church has asked its members to mark Fridays as special, perhaps by giving money to some good cause, or by doing without something they normally take for granted, like meat. This is why Friday has come to be the traditional day to buy fresh fish, or fish and chips.

There does seem to be something solemn about Friday. If someone gives you a "Friday look", it means that he is downcast and sorrowful. It is said to be unwise to marry, put to sea, or begin anything of importance on a Friday. To most people Friday 13th seems particularly unfavourable (except to the Spanish, who avoid Tuesday 13th). This may have a superstitious connection with the fact that there were thirteen at the Last Supper, on the eve of Good Friday.

It is considered best to avoid cutting your hair or nails on Friday, according to a proverb of 1678:

> "Friday's hair and Saturday's horn
> Goes to the devil on Monday morn."

The goddess Frigga, from whom Friday gets its name, was

thought to sit on a float pulled by a pair of cats. This may be the origin of the superstition about its being unlucky for a cat to cross your path on a Friday.

However, Robinson Crusoe must have felt it was one of the luckiest days of his life when he came face to face with another human being on what he had thought was an uninhabited island. Robinson became inseparable from this friend, whom he called "my man, Friday", in honour of the day they met. Sometimes people advertise for a "Girl Friday". This means someone who must be prepared to help by doing any sort of job, just as "Man Friday" did.

Muslims call Friday *Djum'a*, the day of "general assembly". All adult Muslims observe five daily *salāts* or prayer times; on *Djum'a*, the holy day, there is a special service of prayers and then a sermon in the mosque. This takes the place of the usual midday *salāt*. This Friday service is called the *djum'a*, and is so important that it has given its name to the day.

In the Qur'an (or Koran), the Holy Book of the Muslims, it is written: "When ye are called to the Friday *salāt*, hasten to the praise of Allah and leave off your business." This duty to attend the *djum'a* binds every adult male Muslim, even though this holy day is not a day of rest like Sunday for Christians or the Sabbath for Jews.

For cutting your nails:
Cut your nails on Monday, cut them for news;
Cut them on Tuesday, a pair of new shoes;
Cut them on Wednesday, cut them for health;
Cut them on Thursday, cut them for wealth;
Cut them on Friday, cut them for woe;
Cut them on Saturday, a journey you'll go;
Cut them on Sunday, you'll cut them for evil,
For all the next week you'll be ruled by the devil.

Saturday

This is the last day of the week. It is called after Saturn, as you can guess from the Welsh and English names for the day. The German *Sonnabend* (used mostly in South Germany), means "the day before Sunday". Many other foreign names for Saturday mean "Sabbath". The Norwegian name "lørdag" is different from all the others. It means "wash-day" or "bath-day", and was the traditional day for a thorough clean up before one appeared in one's Sunday best.

There always seems to be a cheerful feeling to this first day of the weekend, when fewer and fewer people now have to attend school or work. Most people go on a shopping trip or have some sort of outing. Saturday has also become the customary day for getting involved in sports events – either as a player, or as a spectator on the spot or in front of the television.

The Roman god **Saturn** was known to the Greeks as **Cronos**. He was the father of Jupiter, Juno and several other gods and goddesses. He was a fearsome god who was said to have swallowed many of his children as soon as they were born. Eventually Jupiter (or Zeus, as he was known to the Greeks) put a magic herb into his father's wine, which caused Cronos to spit out the children he had swallowed. They were all alive and furiously angry. They joined forces with Jupiter, Juno and their other brothers and sisters, and waged war against Cronos, eventually getting the better of him and imprisoning him under the earth.

But later, the Romans said that Cronos, or Saturn as they called him, had not been imprisoned, but had taken refuge on earth among them. He had taught them new ways of agriculture, their land had flourished, and peace and plenty had reigned. This became known as the "Golden Age".

So when Romans celebrated the feast of Saturn, (as we saw on page 64), it was a festival celebrating the memory of that

89

glorious golden age, when all men were equal and content. This festival of "Saturnalia" took place towards the end of December and lasted for seven days. It was a time of frenzied feasting and merry-making. Work and business were suspended, and even the slaves enjoyed a holiday, wearing their master's togas and giving orders in his place.

Because Saturn swallowed his children at birth, and so "ate up" their lives, he is sometimes portrayed as an old man holding a sickle, symbolizing Time. In his "Planets Suite", the composer Gustav Holst calls him "The Bringer of Old Age".

Later, in Christian times, the feasts of Christmas and New Year were celebrated over the same mid-winter period as the old Saturnalia.

These days the name Saturn probably means most to us as the name of the series of space launch vehicles developed by the United States from 1958 onward.

The Sabbath

This name for the seventh day of the week comes from the Hebrew word *shabath*, meaning "to rest". Most other European languages have a name for Saturday which originated in this Hebrew word: *subbota* (Russian), *sabato* (Italian), *samedi* (French), *Samstag* (German), etc.

The Bible gives an account of the creation of the world: "On the sixth day God completed all the work he had been doing, and on the seventh day he rested. God blessed the seventh day and made it holy, because on that day he ceased from all the work he had set himself to do."

So the Jews kept the seventh or last day of their week as a day of religious rest. One of the Ten Commandments which God gave them through Moses was a reminder of this: "Remember to keep the Sabbath day holy." During the forty years they spent wandering in the desert, they did no work on the Sabbath, and God provided double the amount of manna (bread from heaven) on a Friday, so that they need not gather food on the following day.

In later times observance of the Sabbath was taken to excessive lengths. Once, when Jesus and some friends were walking through cornfields on a Sabbath, they picked ears of corn and ate them. Some Pharisees, people who were very strict about keeping the Jewish law, asked them why they were doing what was not lawful. On another occasion, when Jesus healed a disabled woman on a Sabbath Day, the ruler of the synagogue – the Jewish place of worship – rebuked him and said there were six other days when such work would be permissible. Jesus himself always stressed that "the Sabbath was given to man, not man to the Sabbath".

Jews still observe the Sabbath, partly to remember God's day of rest after creation, and partly as a memorial of their escape from slavery in Egypt. The Sabbath lasts from sunset on Friday to sunset on Saturday. In the traditional Jewish home the woman of the house lights white candles at sunset on Friday. A *kiddush* or special blessing is said over a cup of wine, which the family share before breaking the special Sabbath loaf (*challah*). On the following day there are services in the synagogue. In the evening the Sabbath ends with a short ceremony, the *havdala*, which stresses the separation between the holy and the unholy, the light and the dark, the Sabbath and the other days of the week.

Non-Jews (or "gentiles", as the Jews call them) apply the word "Sabbath" to their own traditional day of rest, which is the Lord's Day, Sunday, and they think of it as the first day of the week, not the last (see page 76). A "Sabbath" can also be used to apply to any period of absence from work; John Clare describes a bitter January day, saying:

> *"...in the fields the lonely plough*
> *Enjoys its frozen sabbath now..."*

A "sabbatical year" is a year for which one is given leave of absence from one's usual place of work.

This is a rhyme which French children sing in order to help them remember the order of the days of the week:

1. Lundi *matin, l'empereur, sa femme et le petit prince*
   sont venus chez moi pour me serrer la pince.
   Comme j'étais parti, le petit prince a dit:
   "Puisque c'est ainsi, nous reviendrons mardi."

2. Mardi *matin, l'empereur, sa femme et le petit prince*
   sont venus chez moi pour me serrer la pince.
   Comme j'étais parti, le petit prince a dit:
   "Puisque c'est ainsi, nous reviendrons
   mercredi."

3. Mercredi...
4. Jeudi...
5. Vendredi...
6. Samedi...
7. Dimanche...

("On Monday morning, the emperor, his wife and the little prince came to my house to shake me by the hand. As I was out, the little prince said: 'That being so, we shall come back on Tuesday'. On Tuesday morning, etc...")

LUNDI MATIN

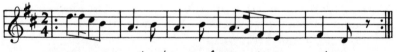

1. Lundi matin, l'emp'reur, sa femme et le p'tit prin-ce
sont venus chez moi — pour me serrer la pin-ce

Mais comme j'étais par -ti, "Puisque c'est ainsi, nous reviendrons mardi."
Le petit prince a dit:

93

Laurentia

Laur - ent - ia, lie - be - Laur - ent - ia mein, Wann werd'n wir wieder bei-
Ach, wenn es (doch) erst wieder Montag wär, Und ich bei meiner Laur -

sammen sein? Am Mo — n — tag
ent - ia wär, Laur - ent - ia wär

This is a song which German children learn when they start school. It helps them remember the days of the week. Every time they mention the name of the girl Laurentia, or one of the days of the week, they have to do a "knees bend". It can be a very energetic song!

Laurentia, liebe Laurentia mein,
Wann werden wir wieder beisammen sein? Am *Montag*.
Ach, wenn es doch erst wieder *Montag* wär,
Und ich bei meiner Laurentia wär, Laurentia wär.

Laurentia, liebe Laurentia mein,
Wenn werden wir wieder beisammen sein? Am *Dienstag*.
Ach, wenn es doch erst wieder *Dienstag* wär,
Und ich bei meiner Laurentia wär, Laurentia wär.

...Am Mittwoch...
...Am Donnerstag...
...Am Freitag...
...Am Samstag...
...Am Sonntag...

(Laurentia, my dear Laurentia, when shall we be together again? On Monday. Oh, if only it were Monday again, and I were with my Laurentia, etc...)

Dashing away with the smoothing iron

'Twas on a Monday morning when I beheld my darling,
She looked so neat and charming in every high degree,
She looked so neat and nimble O,
A-washing of her linen O,
Dashing away with the smoothing iron,
Dashing away with the smoothing iron,
She stole my heart away.

'Twas on a Tuesday morning when I beheld my darling,
She looked so neat and charming in every high degree,
She looked so neat and nimble O,
A-hanging out her linen O,
Dashing away with the smoothing iron,
Dashing away with the smoothing iron,
She stole my heart away.

'Twas on a Wednesday morning when I beheld my darling,
She looked so neat and charming in every high degree,
She looked so neat and nimble O,
A-starching of her linen O,
Dashing away with the smoothing iron,
Dashing away with the smoothing iron,
She stole my heart away.

'Twas on a Thursday morning when I beheld my darling,
She looked so neat and charming in every high degree,
She looked so neat and nimble O,
A-ironing of her linen O,
Dashing away with the smoothing iron,
Dashing away with the smoothing iron,
She stole my heart away.

'Twas on a Friday morning when I beheld my darling,
She looked so neat and charming in every high degree,
She looked so neat and nimble O,
A-folding of her linen O,
Dashing away with the smoothing iron,
Dashing away with the smoothing iron,
She stole my heart away.

'Twas on a Saturday morning when I beheld my darling,
She looked so neat and charming in every high degree,
She looked so neat and nimble O,
A-airing of her linen O,
Dashing away with the smoothing iron,
Dashing away with the smoothing iron,
She stole my heart away.

'Twas on a Sunday morning when I beheld my darling,
She looked so neat and charming in every high degree,
She looked so neat and nimble O,
A-wearing of her linen O,
Dashing away with the smoothing iron,
Dashing away with the smoothing iron,
She stole my heart away.

Somerset folk song

ROMAN NUMERALS

Roman numerals are often used in inscriptions, particularly on old monuments, clocks or gravestones, and sometimes on the title pages of old books. Letters were used to represent numbers.

1	I	16	XVI
2	II	17	XVII
3	III	18	XVIII
4	IV	19	XIX
5	V	20	XX
6	VI	21	XXI
7	VII	50	L
8	VIII	60	LX
9	IX	70	LXX
10	X	90	XC
11	XI	100	C
12	XII	500	D
13	XIII	900	CM
14	XIV	1000	M
15	XV	1900	MCM

A line over a numeral multiplies it by 1000, so $\overline{\text{IV}}$ = 4000

MDCCXIV = 1714
MCMXLIII = 1943
MCMLXXXV = 1985

Other Latin words are still used in phrases about time.
ante means "before"
post means "after"
meridies means "noon", so:

ante meridiem (a.m.) is the time from midnight to noon: morning

post meridiem (p.m.) is the time from noon to midnight: afternoon

ᑕᓍ ABBREVIATIONS ᓍᑐ

Sometimes abbreviations are used in connection with dates on the calendar.

B.C.—before Christ. Julius Caesar first invaded Britain in 55 B.C.

A.D.—*anno Domini*: in the year of Our Lord, that is, within the Christian era. The battle of Hastings took place in A.D. 1066.

A.H.—*anno Hegirae*: in the year of the hejira. Muslims reckon time from the year of Muhammad's flight to Medina from his enemies in Mecca, his "hejira". 16th July 622 in the Julian calendar is fixed as the first day of the year in the Muslims' Holy Book, the Qur'an (Koran).

A.M.—*anno mundi*: year of the world. Jews reckon time from the beginning of man's history as recorded in their traditions.

Books which Tell You More about the Days and the Months

Highdays and Holidays by Margaret Joy (Faber and Faber Ltd.)
Festivals and Saints' Days by Victor J. Green (Blandford Presss)
Myths of the Norsemen ⎫ by Roger Lancelyn Green (Puffin
Tales of the Greek Heroes ⎭ Books, Penguin Books Ltd.)

The Lost Gods of the English by Brian Branston (Thames and Hudson)

Whitaker's Almanack (published annually)

Here's the Church by Peter Watkins and Erica Hughes (Julia MacRae)

Here's the Year by Peter Watkins and Erica Hughes (Julia MacRae)

Special days and months, seen through the eyes of a Gloucestershire boy:
Cider with Rosie by Laurie Lee (Penguin Books Ltd);

an Oxfordshire girl:
Lark Rise to Candleford by Flora Thompson (Oxford University Press);

a Derbyshire farmer's daughter:
The Country Child by Alison Uttley (Puffin Books, Penguin Books Ltd.);

a Northamptonshire country poet:
The Shepherd's Calendar by John Clare (Oxford University Press);

a small boy in South Shields, County Durham:
The Only Child by James Kirkup (Pergamon);

a Welshman:
Quite Early one Morning by Dylan Thomas (J. M. Dent and Sons Ltd.)

ᕦ INDEX ᕤ